THE TRAIN OF THOUGHT
Dreams

Richard Dardis

The Reading Glass Books
1-888-420-3050
www.readingglassbooks.com
fulfillment@readingglassbooks.com

Table of Contents

Welcome back.

When we left last, our champion scientists were being lauded for their genius and their commitment to the health of the Planet Earth and its inhabitants. Upon leaving, our author and the main character were chasing each other through the strawberry fields trying to make a trade, a ride to 2022 for the microphone to sing to the crowd. Neither wanted to yield. The story will not continue because I need to go back to 2022, it's my home. The little man with the gray beard had better give me transportation so I can sign the agreement to get published. Otherwise, we get no public support for our quest.

Obviously, he relented. But…so did I.

And he's up on the stage assuming the part of Taylor Swift and entertaining the crowd. That's what we get for him being lonely for fourteen billion years.

So, the story continues in 2010. The Scientists, Stephen Hawking, Michio Kaku, Neil deGrasse Tyson, and Jim Al Khalili, have left the celebration and are sitting and conferring on how to best tackle the problem. Michio says, "I really think our widespread jamboree today will help us to get the point across about the problem for us and the future of earth. Now we need governments to step up everywhere."

Stephen says, "Except the audience were people who have come and gone. I hope I can be here when the time comes that we are successful. There is no need to continue to manufacture any more war machine implements. Diplomacy and dialogue are the key, period."

Neil adds, "So, we start tomorrow with an aggressive anti-war message everywhere."

To which Michio states, "So what about the 'Train of Thought' and its capabilities? We can't just let it be discovered a million years from now as an anthropological relic."

"Good point Michio; this is one heck of a cosmic traveler. Let's have a real discussion with Taylor Swift over there, when she's done performing and get to the bottom of this thing now," spoke Jim.

"TWEEEET, Taylor, when you're done entertaining, we need to talk to you," spoke Jim.

"One more song honey," responded Yes. One song and twenty-five minutes of encore later and Yes asked, "Okay guys, what's up?"

"Sir we need to have a serious conversation, again," replied Michio.

"We need everything you haven't told us about the future, and the 'Train of Thought'," added Stephen. "And now!"

"Okay men, relax. Was I sexy or what?"

"Taylor was, and you are about to get jumped by four gnarly guys right now buddy, if you don't come clean with some answers," said Neil.

"Okay, okay, Let's just take a breath and calm down," said Yes.

"Everybody sit and I will put the pieces together, okay? Alright, here it goes. When I was seventeen, it was a very good year."

"Knock it off, hairball, and get serious," Jim complains.

"Alright where do you want me to start?"

"How about the earth's demise? Let's start there," answered Michio.

"What about it?" asked Yes.

Neil gives a boot to Yes.

"Okay, okay, the demise is the result of the next world war," said Yes.

"When will that be?" asked Michio. "I can't tell you," Yes responded.

"Why not?" Neil asks.

"Because of my oath," Yes revealed.

"Oath to who?" Jim asks.

"Myself and… and… and.., I can't tell you," Yes squirms.

"Why not?" Michio asks.

"She'll kill me," Yes squirms again.

"She? Who's she?" Jim queries.

"Leave it alone, okay?" says Yes.

"HMMMMMMMMMMMM, so, our little dwarf friend has a girlfriend huh?" Michio adds.

"No, it's not like that," denies Yes.

"Then, what's it like?" asks Jim.

"I'm sorry I cannot divulge anything else about that. What else do you want to know?" Yes asks.

"The 'Train of Thought', could we use it to combat war?" asked Stephen.

"Very easily, you have no idea the power it has. No-one from earth could occupy it and use it for destruction, I can promise you that," Yes stated.

"Could you?" asked Michio.

"Yes, I could, very simply. You saw its power."

"Then, we could hire you to compel nations to stop any thought of war by demonstrating its power, couldn't we?" Neil asked.

"Maybe. But I took an oath to more than myself, remember?" spoke Yes.

"You know more about the train's functions than you let us know before, huh?" Neil asked.

"Yes, I do," Yes said.

"Like what?" asked Neil.

"The fuel sources." Yes said.

"What is it?" questioned Michio.

"Atoms, but the formula I do not know. And that's the truth," Yes replied.

"Atoms!!! So, you invite nearly dead people on board, let them die, and collect their atoms for fuel?"

"No, it's not like that at all. Let me explain, okay? Around two billion years ago, or maybe it was less than that, I was hit by some space junk. The transport developed a minor leak in the fuel tank. I was about to be floating forever, and out of fuel, when I encountered Earth. I landed here and the rest is history," Yes revealed.

"Using my operating system my father provided for me, I was able to seal the leak, but in doing that I must have damaged the fuel replacement system somehow. The repair had to be done from the outside. I put on the outdoor gear from the equipment closet and the problem was solved. It was the first time I was able to leave the transport in 12 billion years. I loved Earth so much I decided to stay. I knew my survival system on the transport was stable, so why leave? I must admit, the last two billion years have been glorious. I watched the most magnificent geological happenings. Imagine your Mount Everest not being there. Better yet watching it rise. Or, the separation of the continents; dinosaurs roaming everywhere. This place called

Earth is the greatest form of an evolutionary spectacle imaginable, and I was here to watch so much of it."

"When humans started to develop, I watched a new life-form slowly evolve. Imagine that? Once I saw that, I knew this planet was the place for me. I have had the greatest of time, seeing all of that. However, as the slow burn of selfishness and greed came along, I lost some interest. Especially when there is so much for all to share. Imagine 30 to 60 thousand people having this entirely to themselves."

"Can we ask you more, please?" asked Neil.

"Of course," offered Yes.

"When you were roaming the universe and watching it grow, what was that like?"

"Well, remember, I was young and new to any of this. I was mostly in fear. All those comets, nebulae and matter floating at me all the time. It was pretty scary. The transport was pretty much indestructible though."

"We can only imagine. Well not any longer huh?" added Michio.

"What I like best is a book that's at least funny, once in a while. What really knocks me out is a book that, when you're all done reading it, you wish the author that wrote it was a terrific friend of yours and you could call him up on the phone whenever you feel like it. That doesn't happen much, though," spoke J.D. Salinger.

Lena Horne added, "I disconnected myself to shield myself from people who would sway to my songs in the club and call me 'N———' in the street. They were too busy seeing their own preconceived image of a negro woman. The image that I chose to give them was a woman who they could not reach therefore, can't hurt."

Dennis Hopper spoke, "I've been sober now for 18 years. With all the drugs, psychedelics, and narcotics I did, I was {really} an alcoholic. Honestly, I only used to do cocaine so I could sober up and drink more. My last five years' of drinking was a nightmare. I was drinking a half gallon of rum with a fifth of rum on the side, in case I ran out, 28 beers a day, and three grams of cocaine just to keep me moving around. And I thought I was doing fine because I wasn't crawling around drunk on the floor."

Gary Coleman said, "I can see through almost any scam, especially one perpetrated by the government. I can see through it…they can't pull the wool over my eyes: it's absolutely freaking' impossible to pull the wool over my eyes about the government."

John Wooden adds, "Be more concerned with your character than your reputation, because your character is what you really are, while your reputation is merely what other people think you are."

On January 27, 2010, author J.D. Salinger passed away. His photo is hanging in the Literary Car. Then, on May 9, Lena Horne passed away; her photo is hanging in the Entertainment Car. On May 28, actor Gary Coleman passed away; his photo is hanging in the Entertainment Car. The next day, May 29, actor Dennis Hopper passed away; his photo hangs in the Entertainment Car. And on June 4, Coach John Wooden passed away; his photo hangs in the Immortals' Car and the Athletic Car, all in the 'Train of Thought'.

2

Albert Einstein

The scientists are continuing to press the Maharishi for more information. He continues to be reluctant to come completely transparent. Michio asks, "Please tell us everything you know. If you had been completely transparent with Albert and the others, we may have been clear of these obstacles."

"I'm being as clear as I know how to be," said Yes.

"Do you trust us completely?" asked Jim.

"Yes, I do. But I don't want to make any mistakes," replied Yes.

"Explain yourself please. What mistakes?" added Neil.

"Any, I just want everything to be okay. I can't allow myself to give too much for fear of the typical human overreaction."

"Sir, we will not overreact, it's under-reaction that's the driving thought here. That's why we need everything you know," spoke Michio.

"Okay, what else do you want to know?" spoke Yes.

"Everything you know. We need to circumvent the Earth's problems you've always spoke of," said Neil.

"Okay, one thing is the absolute negative use of nuclear arms and nuclear reactors. They are time bombs. If opposing forces decide to either use nuclear arms or destroy nuclear facilities, its game over. Also remember, the continents are still moving and shifting. Any of these shifts could cause catastrophic damage to nuclear facilities as well. Nuclear power and heat are the answer to many of Earth's needs, but it is also the catalyst to total-destruction. All scientists know this.

Again, the problem isn't the good guys," the Maharishi spoke. "You all know these variables. But evil lurks and you know that too."

"Do you know of any counter actions to take against nuclear proliferation?" asked Jim.

"The destruction of my universe was due to science way beyond yours. Not being a scientist, I can't say yes or no. I need to do the research in my operation center. I will and I will get back to you on that question."

"That would be a great help sir." spoke Neil.

Jim asks, "Could we sit in with you sir to maybe understand with you?"

"I don't know what good that would do, you wouldn't understand the language."

"But you could translate it to us," responded Jim.

"Remember, my family left me with instructions. Any misuse or miscalculation and the transport may respond to unwanted aliens. I must consult the operating system in depth first, to find if there is any answer to these queries. If we make any mistakes in the transport, it could self-destruct. I will get back to you soon," and Yes vanishes.

3

Max Planck

Sitting and chatting in a booth are Eddie Fisher, Gloria Stuart, Barbara Billingsley, Leslie Nielsen, and Jill Clayburgh.

Eddie states, "By the time I was thirty-three years old I'd been married to both America's sweetheart and America's femme fatale and both marriages ended up in scandal. I'd been one of the most popular singers in America and had given up my career for love. I had fathered two children and adopted two children, and rarely saw any of them. I was addicted to methamphetamines, and I couldn't sleep at night without a huge dose of Librium. And from all this I had learned one very important lesson: There were no rules for me. I could get away with anything, as long as that sound came out of my throat."

Leslie Nielsen adds, "I have always loved science fiction. One of my favorite shows is 'Star Trek.' I liked the trips, where it drops my mind off, because they give you a premise and all-of-a-sudden, you say, 'Oh' and I'm fascinated by it."

Barbara Billingsley pines in, "I feel that I can't do certain things that have been sent to me, scripts, because I think that really- I've been June Cleaver for so many years, because we went back, you know, and we did- 20-year hiatus we had-and we went back and made one hundred and five new ones. And so, I really feel very strongly that there are certain things I won't do."

Gloria Stuart speaks, "I wanted to be a theater actress, but I thought it would be easier to get to New York and the theater if I had a name than if I just walked up the streets as a little girl from California."

Jill Clayburgh offers, "I don't theorize too much. I sort of let the experience sink in, and I have to discover what the character is by doing it and having those thoughts that she's thinking."

The Maharishi has spent many weeks tracking down an answer for the men. He calls the group together for another meeting. They all meet in the locomotive this time.

"Come on in men, it's nice to see you all again. I think I may have the answers for you."

He opens a compartment no-one has ever seen before.

"Men this part of the transport is sacred, please be very careful. Everything is quite delicate in here."

"I have researched as much as I could in the last months. Please sit and listen as I translate to you the answers we are looking for. Or ask questions as well."

Jim asks, "Can you stop and start the machine for inquiries as we go?"

"Yes, I have complete control. Okay simulator can you please tell me about the self-destruct mode of the ship? Oops, wrong language. "Q6uyrtiufigecohf i7tyg8unris liux mjnhbvyoi5v w;omf3xwl," Yes asks.

"9m0v8k-dx;8omnyv;06h5b9um0cliun yfcqliun4cqm."

"It said, if any being attempts to commandeer the transport other than myself it is programmed to destroy itself. And it is irreversible."

"VD^UI&B*ONL;o,;lkerwlimo5eioj0p,-b6[v5to4rinp90-[7jo kjihou4wa9p809pi6bv2-3q74."

"It also says that it recognizes aliens aboard the vessel and approves your entry because of the research and communications I have already conducted. Any other breach without authorization and the entrants will be terminated."

"We never intend on anything of that nature, please explain it to the simulator," spoke Michio.

"Okay, what question do you have for it?" spoke Yes.

Stephen asks, "Could you explain the physics behind the fuel system and how it operates so swiftly through space."

Maharishi asks, "ih5copijgcw[pojhgoijmoxzgedikhh5jkp,6hbeoium pj?" "Oietrcpqk,vx nli ku ntdl;khgvqbvohnv iub;otv ;onp."

"The simulator asks you to please refrain from any inquiries about its travel and destruction capabilities. They are secretive and cannot be divulged, ever," said Yes.

"Does the simulator have an answer for our nuclear proliferation question?" asked Neil.

"Xwerhtvr bjytinubvcxtehrjydyfu," Yes asked.

"Louytrewa,jnmbnvcfdguhylikuyhcvbn 4exz srytdvf ubginomnhubgyv."

"It says it detects that your nuclear science is incomplete yet and you must do more research to understand its maximum usage and tune it to perfection."

Neil asks, "What can the transport do to help pave the way to a more docile future, here on earth."

Yes asks, "Oihn84hro4fomut9nfjtsduiuheo6rjgrf98uhnm?"

"The response is Wyub3dnbjv9m ovpjujbp56 om rknlernrioevjmtg vtou. Ihsiuhs i;l,'4rl0=ytv2i0=uyb4rl0=ytv2i0=uyb98h4fi-p;,,0=u-yv2q6h5bo.i0=jb9o,-mnb. The simulator suggests, reaching out to all inhabitants in a clear and deliberate tone of reconciliation and peace, with the clear explanation of eventual worldwide genocide; and possibly very near."

Michio adds, "What does the simulator see presently in our future, for our ecology and surviving our self-imposed destruction."

Yes asks, "Uihb5pomi[5gc wqp,'nboijmoim, ;oiu4c wqiunh37utfs;o?"

The response is, "6hyvybnboijmoim, ;oiu4cwqiunh37ut fs;o6hyvyb km4ejvr."

"The simulator says the cleanup is easy but don't wait too much longer, it's nearing the impasse," spoke Maharishi. "Apparently you have the technology, but you haven't employed it yet. Better get cracking mates."

Jim asks, "Can the simulator guide us to the best diplomatic direction, for us to take with the world leaders?"

Yes asks, "X3lqkcpeojtmgkluhnomiom,mkhjugh,k,jv[,7jbp.[6tvrpo,[ounh7bgeryubihn?"

The response is, "Xt4cxyvu5yc6uvromn. Show them who is boss," Yes responds to the laughter of four intrigued scientists.

"Okay men, now that we have concluded that, I have some very disturbing information of which I am aware. I have known this for just a short time. It is especially disturbing, and I don't know how it will affect you on a personal note or even a political one, but it's best to share it with you all, and now. The clock is ticking toward global disaster of epic proportion. What I am about to disclose cannot ever be exposed until the time is right for its exposure. So please make sure in your hearts and minds you are prepared to hear the worst," expressed Yes.

"Do you all agree to hear what I know and keep it sacred, and then we can discuss the possibilities after?"

"Stephen, you first," Yes suggested.

"Yes, I do want and need to hear what you know. I'm in it for the health of humanity," said Stephen.

"Michio, your thoughts?" Yes asked.

"As I've said before, I'm all in, and also for humanities' sake," Michio added.

"Neil please, your feelings on this?" questioned Yes.

Neil responds with, "I'm a member of this team, so of course."

"And lastly, Jim your opinion?" asked Yes.

"I'm a lifer Yes, so please expand on your words," Jim retorted.

Yes begins his oratory. "Gentlemen, apparently there is more than one wolf in the equation. As I said, I recently stumbled upon this, and it is staggering. Remember when we all went up to the future? We all studied, read, and poked around. At that time, I read about something highly unusual and unexpected. I kept it to myself so I could do more investigating. Of course, you all know of my unique transformation powers; well, I used them, and numerous times, to see if I could prove what I found were true. And it is true, so here it goes and please trust me. I know I've fibbed a lot over the years, but no fibbing here, I swear."

"We have talked of global catastrophe, due to many possible scenarios -nuclear, atmospheric and genocidal, to name the obvious. Well, the real problem is treason. What I mean is, a man in your USA has sold out your country. In doing so, all the above scenarios become integral to the whole. No matter what your courts or congress have history of and future to, this one man is in a position to sell out your country; and it is a man no one would ever expect, ever. And even worse, the man he answers to is complicit. His boss has sanctioned him to do the dirty work for him, which, in essence, conceals the boss from the complicity. Quite a highly intelligent man, this boss."

"Now, do you all want names and dates of the compromise, or should I keep it concealed for now? However, in doing so, it may make the future very bleak."

Stephen offers, "Sir, what you have said here is extremely alarming, and that is without the names. Also, in exposing the truth now, knowing we know the future, wouldn't we be altering destiny if we do bring light to the truth?"

"As usual Stephen, very wise. So, give me options, my friends. Do we just let the negative ball of catastrophe roll on, or do we step in along the way and silently and slowly expose the beast, for who and what they are, and what their intentions may be?"

Stephen asks the others, "Men would you all let me address this please?"

Michio, Neil and Jim all nod in agreement.

"History has proved that money and power are working partners. However, if you three exceptional men allow yourselves a place in this scenario, you will be committing professional suicide, period. I, however, have nothing to lose, period. So please allow me to ponder on this alone and produce a solution, okay?" Stephen presented.

The other three understood exactly how and why Stephen offered this as a start-up solution, and they all agreed.

Yes adds, "Okay guys, I won't divulge any names. However, please keep a close ear to the ground and we will continue to monitor it during our get togethers, okay?"

They all agree and decide to take a step at a time for humanities' sake.

Yes says, "I will explain this to Richard, our author, as well when I see him next."

On September 22, Eddie Fisher passed away. His photo hangs in the Entertainment Car. On September 26, Gloria Stuart passed away; her photo is hanging in the Entertainment Car. On October 16, Barbara Billingsley died and her photo hangs in the Entertainment Car. On November 5, Jill Clayburgh passed away and her photo also hangs in the Entertainment Car. On November 28, Leslie Nielsen passed and his photo hangs in the Entertainment Car. All are in the 'Train of Thought'.

It's the beginning of 2011 and some travelers who are new and some who have traveled before are here to vacate. In the Dinner Car, seated together are Steve Jobs of Apple; Elizabeth Taylor, the actress; Joe Frazier, the ex-heavyweight champion; Bubba Smith, ex- football great; and Osama Bin-Laden.

Bubba Smith says, "You know I'm not a violent person. You have to back off. People sometimes will try you and try you, until you try not to, but you just have to react. Normally I just walk away."

Joe Frazier responds with, "Champions are not made in the ring, they are merely recognized there. What you cheat on in the early light of morning will show up in the ring under the bright lights."

Liz Taylor says, "It is strange that the years teach us patience; that the shorter our time, the greater our capacity for waiting."

Steve Jobs adds, "You can't connect the dots looking forward; you can only connect them looking backwards. So, you have to trust that the dots will somehow connect in your future."

Osama quotes nothing of any intelligence.

On May 2, 2011, Osama Bin Laden is caught and killed. His body was frozen in time and hangs in the Freezer Car of the 'Train of Thought' for all people to pass and kick, beat, spit on, or any other negative action they want for eternity.

Back in the Compartment of Information, the scientists continue to ask for information.

Jim asks, "Are there any other worlds like our Earth, in the universe?"

Yes asks, "Edfg uingmhoj tvyuvlibk tcsd oljyi,j4fcwaoh5 jm07h54v9umh."

The response is "Tyknulb;I,gtvrlufekrtxjbknyl;";iunlmhybkugtvrjb."

"There are other life forms, not of the same composition as humans. Worlds, yes."

Michio asks, "Is our universe of the same physical composition as your universe?"

Yes asks "Oi3298m654c9k0, uh8noqac7livnl5ew5iuy 50vu6uhw5cjw9uhw?"

The response is, "Erwweiortyun.,vmncik5eo;w54ojvc9jy iiumnybo,tvp.r."

"Yes, except our universe was much older and further advanced."

Neil asks, "How much older was your universe than this one, comparatively speaking?"

Yes asks, "4r3cv 84wm9-gv3 kxi7tfhv-,I,hbvujh87vtm0-?"

The response is, "Ouium65beoi,[c5g inyotouiu m65beoi, [c5ginyot760i65 /.,ec."

"Approximately four times older."

Stephen asks, "What suggestions do you have for the people of Earth, and our future?"

Yes asks, "Yjeciung;omp;lfvu63ut4n;, kue4iumbg4.,hg7j g3iuny4vpo5y mciy3nc5 poi,unycwe rtymu,i.o/il,uj mnyhbtyvttyvdu?"

The response is, "po,iunfry twsqarrte duhfrjgkhyujnxexumhvroijmv ijrsaiygiygybgdciniegbybfegwqiuhpl.pl,hu."

"You only live once, care for one another. One of your states is a wolf, be careful of its real intentions. They want domination. And will do whatever it takes to achieve it."

On March 23, 2011, the wonderful actress Elizabeth Taylor passed away and her photo hangs in the Entertainment Car. On August 3, Bubba Smith passed away and his photo hangs in the Athletic Car. On October 5, Steve Jobs passed away and his photo hangs in the Entrepreneurs' Car. On November 7, Joe Frazier passed away; his photo hangs in the Athletic Car. All are in the 'Train of Thought'.

5

Niels Bohr

The beginning of the new year of 2012 brings us another Presidential race. The war in Syria continues to take countless lives. Over 2000 U.S. soldiers have died in Afghanistan. The U.S. consulate in Benghazi Libya was attacked and Ambassador Chris Stevens and three other courageous men died.

The five appointees are huddled in the transport and still discussing the future.

Michio speaks, "All my years in science, and I was kind of befuddled in there."

Jim says, "That goes for me, too. With all there is and was, I was somewhat lost."

Neil states, "Imagine, we were trained to ask questions and research, and that's all we asked."

Stephen says, "Don't sell yourselves short fellows, the questions were great questions, the answers were also great. But what could we have asked that we don't already know? The simulator answered the questions we asked. What else was there, the contents of nebulae? We are intelligent men, we know the solution, and the Maharishi has been telling us all along, it's the scoundrels. It's all of the white collar, blue collar, no collar, and gold collar that need our attention."

"Very well put Stephen, I am amazed at your brilliance," spoke the Maharishi.

The others all nod in agreement.

"So, where from here men?" asks Michio.

The Maharishi suggests, "How about another jamboree, I just loved being Taylor Swift."

"You are always the alien of humor, aren't you?"

"Bop, bop aloo bop, tutti Frutti, oh Rudy," Yes sings. The others just laugh to the core.

Etta James, Whitney Houston, Mike Wallace, Donna Summer, and Ray Bradbury are having a nice talk.

Etta says, "When I look out at the people and they look at me and they're smiling, then I know I'm loved. That is the time I have no worries, no problems."

Whitney responds, "When I decided to be a singer, my mother warned me I'd be alone a lot. Basically, we all are. Loneliness comes with life."

Mike Wallace responds with, "I was so low that I wanted to exit. And I took a bunch of pills, and they were sleeping pills. And at least they would put me to sleep, and maybe I wouldn't wake up and that was fine."

Donna Summer adds, "Well I'll say that I have an incredible ability to fantasize; I really do. I don't have to have things tangible to be able to see them, and therefore I enjoy so many things, because they're in my mind."

Ray Bradbury adds, "Looking back over a lifetime, you see that love was the answer to everything. The years go by. The time, it does fly. Every single second is a moment in time that passes. And it seems like nothing- but when you're looking back…well, it amounts to everything."

In the booth next to those wonderful people are Andy Griffith, Sally Ride, Neil Armstrong, and Michael Clarke Duncan.

Andy says, "I'm not as good a singer as I am an actor. So that's why I tell the stories I like so much, because I've been a storyteller for a long time. I started as a singer and found out I didn't have a very good voice. That's the reason I went into acting."

Sally Ride speaks, "Science is fun. Science is curiosity. We all have natural curiosity. Science is a process of investigating. It's posing questions and coming up with a method. It's delving in."

Neil Armstrong adds, "Research is creating new knowledge, mystery creates wonder and wonder is the basis of man's desire to understand."

Michael Clarke Duncan adds, "I came along during that time when music, to me was really music. It wasn't about talking about a woman and calling them a derogatory name or something like that. It was real music."

The group has disbanded for a while to 'do their jobs'.

The Maharishi is in his operation center, exploring more relevant answers and solutions. He says to himself, "I was asked to embark on this mission, and I don't think I've succeeded. I wonder what I've missed. I know all the scientists have worked very hard and committed themselves 100%. What can I do to help more? Is it altering destiny if I disguise myself and plug in with the world leaders? I just don't know. I'll have to sleep on it and maybe I'll have an answer tomorrow."

Its January 20, 2012, and Etta James passed away. Her photo is hanging in the Entertainment Car. On February 11, the great Whitney Houston died. Her photo is Hanging in the Entertainment Car. A few months later, on April 7, Mike Wallace passed away; his photo hangs in the Journalist Car. On May 17, Donna Summer passed away; her photo is hanging in the Entertainment Car. Shortly after, on June 5, Ray Bradbury passed away. His photo is hanging in the Literary Car. On July 3, Andy Griffith passed away; his photo hangs in the Entertainment Car. On July 23 of that year, Sally Ride passed away. Her photos are hanging in the Scientific Car and the Courageous Car. On August 25, Astronaut Neil Armstrong passed away; his photos hang in the Courageous Car and the Immortals' Car. Then, on September 3, Michael Clarke Duncan passed away. His photo hangs in the Entertainment Car; all are in the 'Train of Thought'.

On December 14, 2012, Adam Lanza killed his mother Nancy, and proceeded to enter an elementary school in Sandy Hook, CT and mow down twenty beautiful and defenseless children and six adults. Those twenty-six persons' photos are hanging in the Innocent Car, and the Immortals' Car of the 'Train of Thought'.

Its 2013 and the President has been sworn in again. The world is still reeling from the 2008 banking crisis. That in itself seems like a regular occurring event that needs to be handled somehow. At a booth in the Executive Car are General Margaret Brewer, Stan Musial, Margaret Thatcher, Dr. Joyce Brothers, actor James Gandolfini, Astronaut Scott Carpenter, and ex-President Nelson Mandela, who opens with, "Education is the most powerful weapon, which you can use to change the world."

Margaret Thatcher adds, "I'm in politics because of the conflict between good and evil, and I believe that in the end, good will triumph."

Scott Carpenter states, 'We've got to take care of the resources we have on this planet, because there's no resupply possible."

General Margaret Brewer responds, "I never considered any other service… My mother insists I was singing the Marine hymn when I was only five years old."

Dr. Joyce Brothers adds, "The person interested in success has to learn to view failure as a healthy inevitable part of the process of getting to the top."

Stan Musial says, "What I do is never to try and hurt anybody else, and figure if I don't, then I'm not likely to get hurt myself."

James Gandolfini adds, "It's a dark, dark world. If you're going to be in a dark world, I can't think of any better one to be in. I still think I'm lucky to be in it."

The Maharishi summons the scientists to the 'Train or Thought' again, the Caboose this time. As he starts to speak, Stephen cuts in on the conversation. "Yes, men, I have an announcement to make. Please don't be angry with me, but I must call it quits. I just don't have what it takes to continue. I truly want to thank all of you for your friendships and dedication to all things good. Most of all to our experiences together. You men and the men before you are all great, great men. I thank you all. Maharishi I truly want to thank you for bringing me aboard this endeavor. It has been one heck of an experience working with you and traveling with you, and I thank you sincerely."

The Maharishi responds, with tears on his face, "Stephen, you are the most courageous man I have known. We all here, have wondered how you continued for so long with your illness. We want to also thank you sincerely. And we love you."

Michio, Neil and Jim, all with tears on their faces, nod and agree with Yes. They all offer their love and support and wishes for good health.

"Stephen, do you mind staying during our meeting, I have things to say to the group?" asked Yes.

"Of course, I love you guys."

"Great, so men before I blab, do any of you have any ideas?"

"I do Yes. After our last meeting, I thought deeply about this whole history, and I have concluded that what Stephen had said about the scoundrels was 100% correct and that's the message we need to bring out, clearly and succinctly." Neil adds, "And that includes the scoundrels of government, all governments. We need to clean up the dirty laundry."

"Okay guys, cleaning up the dirty laundry is an absolute necessity. I have learned from my efforts that there is someone in your government or your country aiming to destroy it for personal gain. I will do more research, but this is the negative direction that may hurt the planet worse, because, if America gets into a war with other countries due to the compromise this gentleman has done, there will be a global war."

"A mighty large task, but the message is clear," adds Jim.

The Maharishi says, "Men I don't think you guys should jeopardize your careers. That's why I called this meeting. If you get too vocal, you will be putting your careers and lives in jeopardy, and we, and more importantly, your families cannot have that. So, it's up to me and the 'Train of Thought' to be the voice."

On January 2, 2013, the first woman to become a Marine Brigadier General, Margaret Brewer passed away and her photo hangs in the Military Car. On January 9, Stan Musial passed away. His photo hangs in the Athletic Car. A few months later, on April 8, Margaret Thatcher passed away, and her photo hangs in the Diplomats' Car. On May 13, Dr. Joyce Brothers passed away, and her photo hangs in the Medical Car. On June 19, Actor James Gandolfini passed away. His photo hangs in the Entertainment Car. In the fall of that year, on October 10, Astronaut Scott Carpenter passed away and his photo hangs in the Heroes' Car and the Military Car. On December 5, President Nelson Mandela passed away, and his photo hangs in the Freedom Car and the Immortals' Car, and all are in the 'Train of Thought'.

7

George Gamow

Back in the Caboose, the Maharishi continues his conversation with the men. "So, if I were to get aggressive and take on many global personalities to squirm my way into the heads of state, do you guys think I could manage to convince the powers to slowly ease out of the problems that have been created?" asked Yes.

Michio speaks, "As a committed scientist and pacifist, I would beg you not to use coercion in any way. We must play this by the book."

Neil adds, "I completely agree with Michio. Most of what is the problem was created by coercion and misdirection. By the book is my advice."

Jim speaks, "Although I've been with the group the shortest time, I must concur, we cannot take any other approach, other than honesty and integrity. Otherwise, we are also complicit in the same way. "

"Thank you all for your input, and your integrity, I know why you are all in this group. So, what to do and how to do it?" spoke the Maharishi.

"I say we get to the present of the future, in which the books are written and published. We use them as a fortress, and a message of international communication and coordination. And like in the sixties, we band the world together and have peace and anti-war movements. If billions get on the band wagon, globally, our message must be heard and dealt with," opined Stephen Hawking. "But for now, we continue to speak softly and add more voice as time progresses."

"Stephen, that sure didn't sound like retirement!" spoke Michio.

"You never cease to amaze us all, my friend," said Neil.

Jim adds, "Brilliance never retires."

Yes states, "I remember when I recruited you in England that day, I knew you were a gem. Before you completely retire there is something I want to share with all of you in the main transport."

"So, the timeline is approximately eight to nine years of planning and spreading," spoke Jim.

"How will the author know of our plans?" asked Neil.

"Leave that up to me my friends," said Yes. "I will make sure he gets the message. Besides, he is the messenger. We are the message purveyors."

The year 2014 has moved in and the strife in Syria is at its height, and ISIS is disrupting the entire Middle East. The world seems to be fraying. People are being beheaded on social media. There are all kinds of school shootings. Ebola becomes a Global health crisis. A 747- airliner destined for Beijing vanishes from the sky with 239 people on board.

Having lunch together in the Entertainment Car are Phil Everly, Pete Seeger, Phillip Seymour Hoffman and Robin Williams.

Phil Everly says, "When we first started recording, it was before rock, so people thought we were hillbilly hicks. That was something we had to deal with; the girls didn't think we were cool, although they did a few years later. We had ducktails and wore peg-leg pants. We looked like rock and rollers."

Pete Seeger asks, "Do you know the difference between education and experience? Education is when you read the fine print, experience is what you get when you don't."

Phillip adds, "The only true currency in this world is what you share with someone when you're uncool."

At this point, Robin Williams says, "Please, don't worry so much… Because in the end none of us have very long on this earth. Life is fleeting. And if you're ever distressed, cast your eyes to the summer sky…and when a shooting star streaks through the blackness… Make a wish and think of me. Make your life spectacular."

In a booth in the Immortals' Car, eating lunch are Shirley Temple, Maya Angelou, Joan Rivers, and Ben Bradlee.

Ben says, "As long as a journalist tells the truth, in conscience and fairness, it's not his job to worry about consequences. The truth is never as dangerous as a lie in the long run. I truly believe truth sets men free."

Maya responds with, "I have a great respect for the past. If you don't know where you've come from, you don't know where you are going. I have respect for the past, but I'm a person of the moment. I'm here, and I do my best to be completely centered at the place I'm at. Then I go forward to the next place."

Shirley Temple said, "When you're a performer you have to please a large audience. When you're in politics you have to please a very large audience too."

Joan Rivers responds with, "Don't follow any advice, no matter how good, until you feel as deeply in your spirit as you think in your mind that the counsel is wise."

The Maharishi came to my new apartment today in Ridgefield, CT. It's November 28, 2022. He won't tell me how he knew where I was. We had a wonderful time together and laughed like two middle school boys. Man, I didn't realize how short four feet four inches was. I'm six feet tall and it was like Shaq O'Neal standing next to Dustin Hoffman. Meaning no disrespect to either of them.

Yes finally tells Richard after all these years about the wolf in the United States' government. Richard is shocked but simply doesn't know what to do about it.

Anyway, we ate and talked, and ate and talked. I had to beat him to the punch and ask him to please not urinate on my toilet seat this time. He suggested to me to try and take a front row seat in the effort to reach all the people in the world. I told him I've always tried to be a leader. But as anyone can tell, I'm not the greatest with words. However, for now, I will reach out to all the readers of my work and say this. Personally, I have had a very tumultuous life. Mostly all has been because of my idealistic wish of and for the world. And only recently, I realized the naivete in that. All I ask is to read the words from the people of the past that were imported for this trilogy of a story. You will recognize the common thread of goodness in all people, yes, all people. Be a piece of thread in that commonality, not the torch that burns it all to hell.

It's January 3, 2014, and Phil Everly passed away; his photo is hanging in the Musicians' Car. Only a couple of weeks later, on January 27, Pete Seeger passed away; his photo is hanging in the Visionaries' Car and the Artistic car. On February 2, Phillip Seymour Hoffman passed away and his photo hangs in the Entertainment Car. Shortly after, on February 10, Shirley Temple passed away; her photo hangs in the Entertainment Car. On May 25 of that year, Maya Angelou passed away; her photo hangs in the Artistic Car and the Dreamers' Car. Later, on August 17, Robin Williams, the creative genius passed away. His photo hangs in the Artistic Car, the Entertainment Car, and the Genius Car. On September 4, Joan Rivers passed away; her photo is hung in the Entertainment Car. In the fall, on October 21, Ben Bradlee passed away; his photo hangs in the Journalistic Car. All of them are in the 'Train of Thought'.

Erwin Chargaff

9

Erwin Chargaff

Entering the year 2015, the Middle East's turmoil still brews. Syria has a very serious refugee crisis, and over 220,000 deaths. Terror struck the Charlie Hebdo magazine offices in Paris France. China's stock market crashed.

Rod Taylor is chatting with Mr. Cub - Ernie Banks, Mr. Spock - Leonard Nimoy and Robert Schuller who asks, "What would you attempt to do if you knew you could not fail? Let your hopes, not your hurts, shape your future."

Rod Taylor says, "I wouldn't dream of selling my work. I'd give them to my friends and to charities. I'd much rather turn down a starring role in a bad picture and do a small role in a very good picture. I'm not doing my work for constant success."

Ernie Banks responds, "It's a beautiful day for a ballgame, let's play two."

Then Leonard Nimoy says, "I'm touched by the idea that when we do things that are useful and helpful - collecting those shards of spirituality - that we may be helping to bring about a healing."

Leslie Gore is sitting with Michael Graves, John Nash, and Omar Shariff and Omar says, "I want to live every moment intensely. Even when I'm giving an interview or talking to people, that's all that I'm thinking about."

Michael Graves adds, "I see Architecture not as Gropius did, as a moral venture, but as invention, in the same way that poetry or music or painting is invention."

Leslie Gore says, "I don't know any other lifestyle. I get up in the morning and I really do feel that the world is my oyster, and start that way, the same as I would if I were preparing to write a song: put a blank piece of paper up on the piano and you go for it."

John Nash adds, "I would not dare to say that there is a direct relation between mathematics and madness, but there is no doubt that great mathematicians suffer from maniacal characteristics, delirium, and symptoms of schizophrenia."

In the table down three rows are B.B. King, Louise Suggs, Yogi Berra, and Natalie Cole.

Natalie says, "I think I am a walking testimony too; you can have scars. You can go thru turbulent times and still have victory in your life."

Louise adds, "Golf is very much like a love affair. If you don't take it seriously it's no fun, if you do, it breaks your heart. Don't break your heart, but flirt with the possibility."

Yogi adds, "I don't know if they were men or women fans running naked across the field. They all had bags over their heads."

And B.B. King added, "Jazz is the big brother of the blues. If a guy's playing blues like we play, he's in high school. When he starts playing jazz it's like going to college, to a school of higher learning."

Having been with the Maharishi enough times now, I truly understand his motivation. Where is the sense of fair play and altruism when a scoundrel strikes? There is none. What compels evil? He traveled trillions of miles, and he wants to help save humanity. I imagine he could be anywhere he pleases, but he is here. Selflessly taking time to teach us the importance of decency and goodness.

"Sir," I asked, "What's the real purpose for your involvement in humanity?"

He looked at me deeply and said, "The same thing as you Richard, idealism. After all, isn't that the purpose of life? To live it, ideally."

On January 7, 2015, Rod Taylor passed away. His photo hangs in the Entertainment Car. On January 23, Ernie Banks passed away and his photo hangs in the Athletic Car. On February 16, Leslie Gore passed away. Her photo hangs in the Entertainment Car. On Feb 27, Leonard Nimoy passed away. His photo hangs in the Scientific Car and the Entertainment Car. On March 12, Michael Graves passed away. His photo hangs in the Artistic Car. On April 2, Pastor Robert Schuller passed away. His photo hangs in the Humanities Car and the Chapel Car. The following month, on May 14, B.B. King passed away. His Photo hangs in the Artistic Car and the Musicians' Car. On May 23, John Nash passed away. His photo hangs in the Genius Car. Not long after, on July 10, Omar Shariff passed away. His photo hangs in the Actors' Car. On August 6, Louise Suggs passed away and her photo hangs in the Athletic Car. On September 2, Yogi Berra passed away and his photo hangs in the Athletic Car. At the end of the year, on December 31, Natalie Cole passed away and her photo hangs in the Entertainment Car. All of them are in the 'Train of Thought'.

10

Carl Sagan

"Ideally, what does that mean? In the 115 years of the passing of these stories, the population has grown from 1.5 billion inhabitants to 7.5 billion inhabitants. I imagine there may be that many different definitions of ideally," Richard responded.

"One would think there should only be one definition of ideally, and 7.5 billion agreements," offered Yes.

"Yes, will you tell me who is the Wolf in our country? Maybe we can do something about this," states Richard.

"I'm sorry Richard. I cannot disclose it because it's been going on for years and we cannot change the destiny. It must be found out soon in the future," replies Yes.

"Thank you for coming back one more time Stephen. Guys, I have a big surprise that I wanted to wait to share but, being that Stephen has decided to retire from the group I wanted him to see my surprise," Yes said. "Come walk with me men." And he unlocks the vault door inside the locomotive to another hidden passageway. "In here is the Incubation/Hibernation area I spoke of once before. Come take a look."

The four scientists gaze down at a being they don't recognize.

"What is that?" asks Jim.

"That my friends, is the other receiver of my oath. She is my future bride. In my universe, people secured their children's mates with other families before birth. She has been here with me since I left on this journey 14 billion years ago. My instructions were to keep her incubated and hibernated until I felt the correct moment in my life to awaken her. Her presence is exactly how I appeared all those years ago. I have decided that's a great way to embark on our program of peace, would be for all of you men and the Mahatma, along with our past geniuses and everybody's wives, to be our bridal party and Richard, our author, to be my best man. What do you all think?"

Michio says, "I'm honored and completely stunned."

Neil says, "Sir I would be so honored to be in your wedding."

Jim says, "Maharishi we are so proud of you, and of course I would be honored."

Stephen is crying his eyes out. "Nothing will make me prouder sir, of course I would."

"Well then let the planning begin. It may take years but, I'll make it all work. Now, who shall I be for my wedding? And who shall my bride be? Well, I guess I have some thinking to do. Now all you guys get out of my vault. Hahahahaha."

11

David Bowie is talking music with Glenn Frey of the Eagles, Prince, Harper Lee, Abe Vigoda, and George Martin. "The truth is there is no journey. We are arriving and departing all at the same time."

Glenn responds with, "People don't run out of dreams, people just run out of time."

Abe Vigoda adds, "I've always been content just to be working and making a modest living for my wife and child."

Harper Lee pines in, "Real courage is when you know you're licked before you begin, but you begin anyway and see it through no matter what."

Prince adds, "Every day I feel is a blessing from God, and I consider it a new beginning. Yeah, everything is beautiful."

So, George Martin adds, "I have lived a thousand lives and I've loved a thousand loves. I've walked on distant worlds and seen the end of time. Because I read."

Muhammed Ali, Elie Wiesel, Gene Wilder, Arnold Palmer, and John Glenn are commiserating and having a drink or two.

Ali says, "I wish people would love everybody else the way they love me. It would be a better world."

Elie adds, "Friendship marks a life even more deeply than love. Love risks degenerating into obsession, friendship is never anything more than sharing."

Gene Wilder speaks, "I trust if your life is right, the right things will happen at the right time. If the chords are in harmony inside, I think other things will happen in the same way. That sounded highfalutin' to me once, but I believe it now."

Arnold adds, "I'm not much for sitting around and thinking about the past or talking about the past. What does that accomplish? If I can give young people something to think about, like the future, that's a better use of my time."

John Glenn adds, "If there's one thing I've learned in my years on this planet, it's that the happiest and most fulfilled people I've known are those who devoted themselves to something bigger and more profound than their own self-interests…"

All the guys head back to the Caboose to have one last group think before Stephen leaves. Stephen opens by saying, "I am beyond words. All those years and he finally comes completely clean. I always felt there was something he wasn't sharing. But I just really love him, that's for sure."

Michio adds, "He is beyond super. I am so, so thankful for him involving me in his life and this expedition, I can't thank him enough."

Neil speaks, "When I was approached for this quest, I was extremely doubtful, but now, I'm overwhelmed with him and all of you."

Jim pines in and says, "I'm the last one to be inducted and I'm also as ecstatic as you all are, I can't imagine how this will end."

On January 10, 2016, the music icon David Bowie passed away; his photo is hanging in the Musicians' Car and the Entertainment Car. The following week on January 18, the great Eagle, Glenn Frey passed away; his photo is hanging in the same two Cars. One week later, on January 26, known as Tessio from the Godfather, Abe Vigoda passed away. His photo hangs in the Entertainment Car. On February 16, the great author, Harper Lee passed away and her photo hangs in the Literary Car. On March 8, the Beatles' great producer George Martin passed away. His photo is hung in the Musicians' Car.

On April 21, musical genius Prince died. His photo hangs in the Musicians' Car. On July 2, Elie Wiesel died, and his photo is immortalized in the Immortals' Car and the Literary Car. On August 29, Gene Wilder passed away, and his photo hangs in the Entertainment Car. Shortly after, on September 25, the great golfer Arnold Palmer passed away. His photo hangs in the Athletic Car and the Humanitarians' Car. On December 8. an American hero John Glenn passed away. His photo's hang in the Congressional Car and the Heroes' Car. All these icons' photos hang in the 'Train of Thought'.

12

"Sometimes you have to know someone really well to realize you're really strangers," spoke Mary Tyler Moore.

Chuck Berry says, "It's amazing how much you can truly learn if your intentions are truly earnest."

So, Don Rickles adds, "If I were to insult people and truly mean it, that wouldn't be funny. There's a difference between an actual insult and just having fun."

Helmut Kohl states, "We humans have an abyss inside us. The more power people have the greater the danger."

Glen Campbell adds, "Success is not getting what you want, it's enjoying what you have."

The comedian Jerry Lewis says, "Every man's dream is to be able to sink into the arms of a woman. Without falling into her hands."

Hugh Hefner adds, "Living in the moment, thinking about the future and staying connected to the past, that's what makes me feel whole."

The immortal Tom Petty suggests, "Do something you really like and hopefully it pays the rent, as far as I'm concerned that's success."

So, Fats Domino says, "Everybody started calling my music rock and roll. But it wasn't anything but the same rhythm and blues I'd been playing down in New Orleans."

"Should we plan a gala event for the Maharishi's wedding and invite the world or should it be a small affair?" Spoke Michio.

"I say we consult him first. However, I don't' think it should be for years," added Neil.

"I agree, let the mates get to know each other in their original form first and that could take many years," offered Jim.

The Maharishi enters the Caboose and says, "Guys, I'm scared. It's been quite a spell since I left home. I haven't spoken to anyone from my past, except No, Eh, and Huh in 14 billion years, what if we don't hit it off? And besides she's still a child. Look at me I'm so old I've seen a universe being born. I've watched stars turn supernova, I played with dinosaurs, then of course there's you earthlings, oh my, you earthlings."

Jim responds with, "Than that should make you prepared for the unification, my friend. Think about what you can teach her? A whole new universe."

Neil adds, "We are all behind you sir. Any questions just ask, we're by your side for anything."

Michio says, "Maharishi, no one is more prepared than you for this marriage. Think about what you know and all your experiences. You 're the king."

"Thank you for all the words of support and comfort guys, you really make me feel great. It's going to be a long while before any marriage though. I haven't told Richard, the author yet, so, if any chance you are with him let me be the one to tell him, okay?"

"You have our word buddy," spoke Michio.

It's the beginning of January 2017 and a new President of the United States is being sworn in, Donald J. Trump. After spending his entire adult life in real estate, America and the world are in for a real test.

On January 25, 2017, Mary Tyler Moore passed away; her photo is hanging in the Entertainment Car. On March 18, rock and roll icon Chuck Berry passed away. His photo hangs in the Musicians' Car. On April 6, Don Rickles passed away. His photo is hung in the Comedians' section of the Entertainment Car. Then, on June 16 Helmut Kohl passed away. His photo hangs in the Diplomats' Car. On August 8 singer Glen Campbell passed away. His photo is hung in the

Musicians' Car. On August 20 comedian Jerry Lewis passed away. His photo hangs in the Comedians' section of the Entertainment Car. On September 27 Hugh Hefner passed away. His photo is hanging in the Entrepreneurs' Car. On October 2, Tom Petty passed away. His photo is hanging in the Musicians' Car. Soon after, on October 24, Fats Domino died, and his photo is hanging in the Musicians' Car, and all are in the 'Train of Thought'.

White nationalists, Neo-Nazis, and members of the alt-right clash with counter-protesters in Charlottesville, Virginia. We face a renewed threat of nuclear war. Robert Mueller is appointed Special Counsel to conduct investigations into Russian interference in the 2016 Presidential Campaign. Tensions with North Korea spark concerns for the nuclear arms issue. What a year!

Moving in to 2018, the tensions between Republicans and Democrats are boiling up as usual. Our Scientists, as usual, are busy with their daily routines of work, husbandry, and fatherhood. The Maharishi is preparing to awaken his bride but is forever worrying about the result. "I just don't know when I should awaken her," he thinks to himself. So, he enters the incubation/hibernation cell of the transport alone. He is standing and just staring at her beauty, remembering the beings in his race and the different look they had to humans.

"What was her name?" He can't recall. He must consult the historical section to remember. "I think I should brush up on my race and language for some time before I awaken her." So, it's off to the archives to study.

13

Richard Feynman

Vic Damone, Billy Graham, Hubert de Givenchy, Stephen Hawking, and Barbara Bush are sitting in a booth in the Lounge, and Barbara Bush starts the conversation. "At the end of your life you will never regret not having passed one more test, not winning one more verdict or not closing one more deal. You will regret time not spent with a husband, a friend, a child, or a parent."

Billy Graham adds, "What is the greatest surprise you have found about life? A university student asked me several years ago. 'The brevity of it,' I replied without hesitation. …Times move so quickly, and no matter who we are or what we have done, the time will come when our lives will be over. As Jesus said, "As long as it is day, we must do the work of Him who sent me. Night is coming when no one can work.""

Hubert de Givenchy says, "Hairstyle is the final tip-off on whether or not a woman knows herself."

Stephen Hawking adds, "Science is not only a disciple of reason, but also one of romance and passion. The past like the future, is indefinite and exists only as a spectrum of possibilities. I never got a chance to expose the wolf the way I promised I would."

Vic Damone passed away on February 11, 2018, and his photo hangs in the Entertainment Car. Billy Graham passed away on February 21, and his photo is hung in the Immortals' Car and the Chapel Car. Hubert de Givenchy passed away on March 10 and his photo is hanging in the Entrepreneurs' Car. Stephen Hawking passed on March 14; his photo hangs in the Immortals' Car, the Scientific Car and the Genius' Car. Barbara Bush passed on April 17, and her photo is hung in the Diplomats' Car, and all are in the 'Train of Thought'.

The Maharishi summons the remaining three men for a meeting. "Men Stephen has passed away. He was such a brilliant man and a crucial part of our group. What should we do? Do we replace him this late in the chase or are we okay with the three of you?"

Michio states, "There is not much time between now and the first publication, I think we are okay to commandeer what's left between us four."

Neil adds, "Yes I agree, considering how much we meet there is really no need for a fourth scientist."

Jim pines in, "Besides we also have a wedding to be a part of."

"Okay It's settled. Remember, I can bring Stephen back with the rest of the past scientists when the wedding is going to happen. I still need an identity for my bride too," said Yes.

"Sir can I tell you something to think about?"

"Yes Michio of course you can."

"Sir in all your travels, how many humans have you encountered?"

"Billions Michio, why?"

"And how many were the same as one another."

"None, of course," Yes replied.

"Then, there you go sir, she needs no-one's identity but her own. In all the times that you played a role of someone else besides feeling sexy, didn't you feel fake and not yourself?"

"You are completely correct Michio and thank you for the advice," Yes stated.

"You see sir too much falsity goes on in our world. Just be yourself, and let your bride be herself, whatever that means to each of you," Michio opined.

Aretha Franklin, Kofi Annan, Burt Reynolds, Stan Lee and George H.W. Bush are all chatting together and the conversation wanes down to Aretha saying, "Music does a lot of things, for a lot of people. It's transporting for sure. It can take you right back, years back, to the very moment certain things happened. Your life is uplifting, it's encouraging, it's strengthening."

Kofi adds, "We may have different religions, different languages, different colored skin, but we all belong to one human race."

Aretha Franklin passed away on August 16, 2018. Her photo is hanging in the Entertainment Car of the 'Train of Thought'. Two days later, Kofi Annan passed away on August 18; his photo hangs in the Diplomats' Car of the 'Train of Thought'.

Burt Reynolds said, "I hate prejudice of any kind, whether it be color or sexual preference." He died on September 6, 2018, and his photo is hanging in the Entertainment Car.

Stan Lee quoted, "There is only one who is all powerful, and his greatest weapon is love." Stan died on November 12, and his photo hangs in the Artistic Car.

George H.W. Bush said, "The American dream means giving it your all, trying your hardest, accomplishing something, and then I'd add to that giving something back. No definition of a successful life can do anything but include serving others." George Bush died on November 30; his photo hangs in the Presidential Car and the Diplomats' Car and all are in the 'Train of Thought'.

14

The year 2019 brings in many dramatic happenings. The awakening of an alien from another universe, although the world is not aware of this phenomenon, eventual worldly outbreak of the Covid-19 virus. The Donald Trump Impeachment process grips the country. Supreme Court appointees are being ridiculed and grilled. There are college admissions scandals. There's the arrest and death of Jeffrey Epstein, the intricate planning of a world-wide plan to rid the world of the big war machine, hate, killings and lack of freedom world-wide. What a task.

On the 'Train of Thought' are James Ingram, sitting with Frank Robinson, John Havlicek, Doris Day, Tim Conway, I.M. Pei, Gloria Vanderbilt, and Toni Morrison.

James says, "Remember the dream, you have a choice, your heart will know, you got to look back sometime to know where to go. You have a voice, long as you live, it's never too small you got to give." He passed on January 13, 2019. His photo hangs in the Musicians' Car of the 'Train of Thought'.

Frank Robinson adds, "It's nice to come into a town and be referred to as the manager of the Cleveland Indians, instead of the First Black Manager." He died on February 7, 2019. His photo hangs large in the Athletic Car of the 'Train of Thought'.

John Havlicek said, "If you are honest with yourself and can look into the mirror and believe that you gave 100 percent, you should feel proud." He passed away on April 25, 2019. His photo hangs in the Athletic Car of the 'Train of Thought'.

Doris Day said, "I like joy; I want to be joyous; I want to have fun on the set; I want to wear beautiful clothes and look pretty. I want to smile, and I want to make people laugh. And that's all I want. I like it. I like being happy. I want to make others happy." She died on May 13, 2019. Her photo hangs in the Entertainment Car of the 'Train of Thought'.

The following day, Tim Conway said, "At first, I wanted to be a jockey. I rode horses in Cleveland, but I kept falling off and I was afraid of horses. So, there wasn't much of a future in it." He passed away on May 14, 2019. His photo hangs in the Entertainment Car of the 'Train Thought'.

Architect I.M. Pei quoted, "Contemporary architects tend to impose modernity on something. There is a certain concern for history, but it's not very deep." He passed away on May 16, 2019. His photo hangs in the Artists' Car of the 'Train of Thought'.

Gloria Vanderbilt quoted, "We are not put on this earth to see through one another. We are put on this earth to see one another through." She died on July 17, 2019, and her photo hangs in the Literary Car of the 'Train of Thought'.

Toni Morrison stated, "And I am all things I have ever loved: scuppernong wine, cool baptisms in silent water, dream books and number playing." She passed away on August 8, 2019, and her photo and writings hang in the Literary Car of the 'Train of Thought'.

The Maharishi has woken his bride. Before he did, he had to return to his original self that he was pre-human. "Oh my, I haven't felt this way for over ten thousand years, longer than that. Let me look at myself in the mirror. OUCH!!! No wait, I'm not bad. Much older, but not bad. What will Blu think?" Blu is his future bride's name given to her by her family.

He taps on the door of the temporary room he has provided for Blu's privacy, in the secret chamber of the transport. She opens the door, and he is immediately awestruck. "Blu, you are so beautiful. Why did I wait so long to awaken you?"

She says, "9unh345-mn8uj54cwm0[9jf3tnu9v48ydr909y8o?"

"I don't understand what you said." In his native language, he says, "8nhcxemp9c ,ckjimop6v3 hpoi, mu875fuybih." (The English translation, "Oh, I'm sorry I haven't spoken our language in a long time. I forgot, sorry.") He adds, "&FFojmnexol,imujngtfredum7jyh656g, meaning, "You look so beautiful, why did I wait so long to awaken you?"

Blu says "YTFB(&*^TN() &NY(* U)PNG FD$#S$W%^&%*(_ {MO{IJB*^ TVFB* ONYG," meaning, "Oh thank you Yes, that's such a nice compliment."

And the courtship begins. Yes takes Blu everywhere in the new universe he can, as a pre-marriage honeymoon - so to speak.

Blu asks, "9uh235uyv2Blu, 9uh23 5uyv2982tviunhj0u8 38umnp3qjmuv8u0," ("Will I ever be able to speak the funny language Yes?")

He replies, "E%CUTV^CYIBOUNGpcE%CUTV^CYIBOUNGpcv 0m9v8yw 08ucm4wgc09um9,0hvvbkmbi7n56uybv." ("It's a really very simple form of communicating, you'll see.")

She says, "n98054v8um04vcfliuhybdr76jm4f9p8 yn4397y." ("Oh that's comforting, it sounds so difficult.")

After some weeks of exploring the universe, they come back to earth to begin planning. Yes calls the scientists to the 'Train of Thought'.

"4fcx,j0-76g98t98j0,g. Oops sorry, I was talking to Blu in our language for weeks and I just realized my mistake. How are you all doing?"

"That's too funny, the guy is in love." Michio adds, "Well isn't that cute, our little hairball world traveler is smitten."

Jim also adds, "There's nothing like a little romance to keep a guy's spirit alive. How was the trip Yes?"

"It was the best, we had such a great time seeing many of the sights of the universe," the Maharishi said.

"But now down to business. What's on the agenda boys?" Yes asked.

Michio states, "Well, while you were gone, we decided to plan for a blowout wedding between Blu and you. Then we are going global with the emphasis on world peace and freedom for all."

Neil adds, "It's going to be an all-out blitz, everywhere. We've already begun notifying our colleagues around the globe for universal support."

Jim says, "It's amazing the amount of people who agree with the tone of peace and unity around the world. I'm getting so excited."

Stephen Hawking

15

Stephen Hawking

It's the beginning of 2020 and another presidential race will be brewing this year. No one knows who the opposing candidate will be. Donald Trump will, of course, be the Republican candidate. Covid-19 is disrupting the world in every way possible. Thousands upon thousands of deaths are happening as a result globally. Countries are forcing lockdowns. People are frustrated. Schools are closed, and students are being taught through the internet. Suicides due to trauma of mental and financial constraints are abundant.

Here on the 'Train of Thought', there are no worries. Everybody is insulated from the problems of life. In a booth talking are football great Gayle Sayers, Baseball immortal Bob Gibson, another baseball immortal Whitey Ford, and another, Joe Morgan.

Gayle says to the baseball men, "I don't care to be remembered as the man who scored six touchdowns in a game. I want to be remembered as a winner in life."

Bob Gibson responds with, "Fishing is one of the greatest things you can do, it has the power to relax you like nothing else and there's nothing quite like the thrill of the catch."

Joe Morgan quotes, "When you're a kid growing up, you say you want to make it to the Major Leagues, and when you reach that dream, that's what it's all about."

Whitey Ford said, "Hell if I didn't drink, or smoke I'd win twenty games every year. It's easy when you don't drink, smoke, or horse around."

In the booth next to them sits Sean Connery, Alex Trebek, Pierre Cardin, and Dawn Wells.

Sean says, "Love may not make the world go round, but I must admit it makes the ride worthwhile."

Alex adds, "It's very important in life to know when to shut up. You should not be afraid of silence."

Then Pierre adds his thoughts, "I was very lucky, I was part of the post war period when everything had to be redone."

Dawn Wells added, "Acting is my first love. Just because a woman is over 50 does not mean she no longer has anything to offer. If anything, we have so much more to offer! We have lived life. We get so much better with age."

"I was thinking of the place we could have a triple ceremony. The first part is to introduce our group of alien friends to the world. The second part, the demanding of an armistice or moratorium, globally on all militaristic arms to every nation on the planet. Third, a closed-circuit viewing globally, of the wedding of Blu and Yes. Of course, including all the scientists and the crew of the 'Train of Thought', No, Eh, and Huh. What do you all think?" Richard asked of the scientists.

"I think that would be a complete success or a total failure. How would the world react to our friends the very first time? Especially Governments. They may commit us all to prisons or nuthouses. Either of which I don't want to end up in." spoke Neil.

Jim adds, "It may have been a spectacular voyage for us but, have we broken any laws, by being involved with extra-terrestrials and not advising our governments?"

Michio asks, "That is one thing that has always stood out in my mind. How do we explain or justify this, coherently, and legally?"

"Okay, why don't we talk to the Maharishi. Maybe he will agree to just the Moratorium?" said Richard.

"I'm right here my friends. You all make extremely valid arguments to our implausible scenario. What should we do?" asked the Maharishi.

Michio opines, "Men we cannot allow ourselves the open door of government scrutinization. We will all be pariahs and outcasts for having participated in this historic coverup. Maharishi, we all love you. You have been a guiding light to all of us. I'm sure our scientific forebearers would agree. To be completely candid, how would the world treat Yes and Blu? That's the most important question of all. Look back on history and how people have treated things they either didn't understand or were in fear of."

Neil adds, "We cannot just stop, we cannot disavow the last ten thousand years or even the last one hundred and twenty. All the efforts to move in a positive direction for mankind would be deemed a failure."

Jim jumps in and says, "Deemed a failure by who? No-one knows except us. The last big ceremony we had was only in front of the people who had passed through the 'Train of Thought'. The Maharishi was Taylor Swift, so she doesn't have any recollection. The same holds true for all the characters of the past that he portrayed. No-one knows anything. I say we have another jamboree and invite all the past participants only. We explain about Yes and Blu and the 'Train of Thought' and just have a great wedding and a wonderful reception."

Richard thinks and adds, "So all the documentation that I have compiled would be just trashed? The first book is already in publication. That was the plan."

Michio responds, "Hold on Richard, that's not true. Your book and the others you have written are all fiction to date. Continue with the publication. As time moves forward, we can always think of ways to introduce our friends in the future. They are not leaving here, like the Maharishi said, this is his home."

"That's a fabulous idea. We can use the power of the 'Train of Thought' in many ways. Both from a book of fiction to reach people, and the real 'Train of Thought' to continue our dream," Richard agrees.

On September 23, 2020, Gayle Sayers passed. His photo is proudly hanging in the Athletic Car. On October 7, Bob Gibson passed away. His photo is also proudly hung in the Athletic Car. October 9 is the date Whitey Ford passed away. His photo is also proudly hung in the Athletic Car. In just a few days, on October 12, Joe Morgan passed away. His photo hangs also in the Athletic Car. And in the same month, on October 31, Sean Connery passed away and his photo hangs in the Entertainment Car. Next month, on November 8, Alex Trebek passed away. His photo hangs in the Entertainment Car. On December 29, Pierre Cardin passed away and his photo hangs in the Entrepreneurs' Car. At the end of the year, on December 30, Dawn Wells passed away and her photo hangs in the Entertainment Car. All of them are in the 'Train of Thought'.

16

Well, it was final, Donald Trump lost the Presidential Election to Joe Biden. It's January 20, 2021, and the United States has a new President. The Covid pandemic is wreaking havoc world-wide. Lockdowns are still in place. Students are still out of school. The death rate has fallen considerably, and the inoculations seem to be easing the strain of the effects of Covid-19. On January 6 of that year, people stormed the Capitol building in Washington D.C. out of anger that they believed the election was stolen. People lost their lives senselessly and sadly.

At a table in the 'Train of Thought', Betty White, Desmond Tutu, Cicely Tyson, Hank Aaron, Sarah Weddington, Michael Nesmith, and Colin Powell are having drinks and chatting.

Betty opens the conversation with, "There's no formula. Keep busy with your work and your life. You can't become a professional mourner. It doesn't help you or others. Replay the good times. Be grateful for the years you had."

Desmond Tutu adds, "If you are neutral in situations of injustice, you have chosen the side of the oppressor. If an elephant has its foot on the tail of a mouse, and you say that you are neutral, the mouse will not appreciate your neutrality."

Cicely Tyson said, "I think when you begin to think of yourself as having achieved something, then there is nothing left for you to work towards. I want to believe there is a mountain so high that I will spend my entire life striving to reach the top of it."

Hank Aaron adds, "I tell young people - including my granddaughter - there is no short cut in life. You have to take it one step at a time and work hard. And you have to give back."

Sarah Weddington responds with, "It is unthinkable to allow complete strangers, whether individually or collectively as state legislators or others in government, to make such personal decisions for someone else."

Colin Powell adds, "If you are going to achieve excellence in big things, you develop the habit in little matters. Excellence is not an exception; it is a prevailing attitude."

Michael Nesmith said, "It's important to be precise about words, because of the thought value of them - they frame so much of the way we understand things."

"So, let us plan the ceremony for New Years Eve on December 31, 2022, that will give us time to coordinate all we need to do for a wonderful gala event. What do you say guys?" said the Maharishi.

"That sounds like a good plan. We won't have to worry about Covid by then and it will let us bring in the New Year with some other unusual events," spoke Jim.

Maharishi says, "I am completely disappointed guys, I was truly hoping we were going to be a showcase for the world. Finally, we would achieve our objective of reaching all of humanity and explaining all the points to the crisis. Is there any way we could compromise?"

Jim responds, "Sir, you heard what we said about the potential for disaster, didn't you? You also witnessed many times in our history how humans and governments react to unknown elements. People die in those scenarios. And you, we don't want that for you and Blu, let alone ourselves. What are your suggestions?"

"I don't have any. I am broken hearted. Imagine that I have been dreaming of the perfect end to this, and now nothing," spoke Yes.

Michio responds "We have some time sir, let's not give up hope yet. Guys, keep your thinking caps on okay."

"Remember in the seventies the group contacted the government? Three different administrations visited the 'Train of Thought' and all three failed us. We can't fail humanity," the Maharishi added.

On January 22, 2021, Hank Aaron Passed away. His photo is hanging in the Athletic Car. On January 28, Cicely Tyson passed away her photo hangs in the Entertainment Car. On October 18, Colin Powell passed away and his photo hangs in the Military Car and the Diplomats' Car. On December 10, Michael Nesmith passed away. His photo hangs in the Musicians' Car. On December 26 Sarah Weddington passed away and her photo hangs in the Legal Car. Also, on December 26 Desmond Tutu passed away. His photo is hanging in the Diplomats' Car. On Dec 31 Betty White passed away and her photo is hung in the Entertainment Car and all of them are in the 'Train of Thought'.

17

Michio Kaku

"Richard….."

It's the beginning of 2022, and the group is in full advance mode to find the solution to their dilemma. On the 'Train of Thought' are Ray Liotta, Naomi Judd, Thick Nhat Hanh, Michael Lee Aday (Meatloaf), Charles McGee, Sydney Poitier, Queen Elizabeth, Peter Bogdanovich, Kirstie Alley, Olivia Newton-John, and James Caan.

Queen Elizabeth stated, "The world is not the most pleasant place. Eventually your parents are going to leave you, and nobody is going to go out of their way to protect you unconditionally. You need to learn to stand up for yourself and what you believe and sometimes, pardon my language, kick some ass."

Tuskegee Airman Charles McGee adds, "Our Country is more diverse than it ever has been, … What is the strength of our country? It's the people. If you don't get the best out of everybody, who knows what the country has lost?"

Thick Nhat Hanh adds, "Letting go gives us freedom, and freedom is the only condition for happiness. If in our heart, we still cling to anything - anger, anxiety, or possessions - we cannot be free."

Peter Bogdanovich adds, "I think one of the reasons younger people don't like older films, films made say before the sixties, is that they've never seen them on the big screen, ever. If you don't see a film on a big screen, you haven't really seen it. You've seen a version of it, but you haven't seen it. That's my feeling, but I'm old fashioned."

Ray Liotta states, "I've only been in one fight in my life…in seventh grade. Yet everyone thinks I'm a maniac."

Meatloaf says, "For the past thirty-two years, I've done nothing outside of the entertainment business. I've had some real highs and some real lows, but I love the work so much that I never once thought of quitting."

Naomi Judd offers, "For many people, managing pain involves using prescription medicine in combination with complementary techniques like physical therapy, acupuncture, yoga, and massage. I appreciate this because I truly believe medical care should address the person as a whole - their mind, body, spirit."

To which Sydney Poitier adds, "You don't have to become something you're not to be better than you were. A person doesn't have to change who he is to become better. I simply wake up every morning a better person than when I went to bed. The journey has been incredible from the beginning."

James Caan says, "I think, we have to believe in things we don't see. That's really important for all of us, whether it's your religion or Santa Claus, or whatever. That's pretty much what it's about."

Olivia Newton-John responds with, "You never know what the future holds, so I'm just enjoying being happy, healthy, and having my wonderful husband by my side."

Kirstie Alley completes the conversation with, "When push comes to shove it ain't the science that's going to lift you up - it's the belief, the spiritual side of life, that's going to lift you up no matter…"

"Richard……"

It is the month of September, and the Maharishi is almost complete with his preparations for the nuptials. They haven't concluded on Blu's dress yet, nor the final location of the Gala event. All the past and present scientists have been fitted for tuxedos. The wives' gowns are also in the works. Maharishi asks the men. "Have we forgotten anything?"

Jim says, "I believe we are ready to go pal."

Neil adds, "Yes sir it seems like we're all prepared."

Michio adds, "You've done a fine job of preparing, our friend."

Three more months until the wedding day and all is okay in the group except, the scientists have concluded between themselves that Yes may have some ideas he hasn't shared. Regarding of course, the original intent of exposing the world to the expedition, and the 'Train of Thought'.

Michio whispers to the other two, "I hope he can go thru with the plan of silence."

Neil adds "Well men if not, be prepared for the fallout. It may be disastrous."

Jim says, "No maybes about it. We will have some serious questions to answer."

"Richard….."

On January 2, 2022, Michael Lee Aday, otherwise known as Meatloaf, passed away. His photo hangs in the Musicians' Car. On January 6, Peter Bogdanovich passed away. His photo hangs in the Directors' Car. Also On Jan 6, Sydney Poitier passed away. His photo is hung in the Entertainment Car. Ten days later, on January 16, Charles McGee passed away and his photo hangs in the Heroes' Car and the Military Car. On January 22, Thick Nhat Hanh passed into another world. His photo is hanging in the Immortals' Car. On May 26, Actor Ray Liotta Passed away. His photo hangs in the Entertainment Car. Naomi Judd passed away on May 30. Her photo is hung is the Entertainment Car. On July 6, Actor James Caan passed away. His photo is hanging in the Entertainment Car. On August 8, beloved actress and singer Olivia Newton-John passed away. Her photos are hanging in the Musicians' Car and the Entertainment Car. On September 8, the world is saddened by the passing of Queen Elizabeth. Her photos are hanging in all the Cars. On December 5, Kirstie Alley passed away and her photo is hanging in the Entertainment Car, and all are in the 'Train of Thought'.

"Richard….."

It is the day of the nuptials, and everyone is excited and ready. We have on hand, Albert Einstein, Max Plank, Niels Bohr, Erwin

Chargaff, George Gamow, Carl Sagan, Richard Feynman, Stephan Hawking, Michio Kaku, Neil deGrasse Tyson, Jim Al Khalili and Mohandas K. Gandhi, along with Eh, No, and Huh. Blu is gorgeous, and the Maharishi has never looked sexier. Don't tell him that.

The location the Maharishi and Blu chose for the nuptials is on the beaches of Negril in Jamaica, a stunning sight and beautiful scenery. The Captain of the Titanic, Captain Edward J. Smith has the honors of performing the nuptials.

Everyone is ready and Liberace is playing the wedding song on his Grand Piano.

It's Nov 6, 1961, **"Richard…. will you wake up please, you have to go to school."**

"But Mom, can I please stay home today. I was having such a great dream."

"No, your father took Susan and Ronnie already, now get up and get ready for school. Your breakfast is on the table," his mom spoke.

"Man, I guess I'll try and see you folks tonight, after I fall asleep. If not, have a great honeymoon, you two. Love you. I can't wait until 2022. To see what happens."

18

It is the actual day of Dec 31, 2022, at 1:14 pm. I am extremely anxious, as I have been for the last 61 years, to go to sleep tonight in the hope of finally completing the dream I was in the middle of on Nov 6, 1961. If my mom had only let me sleep that morning, we may already know the results of our quest for world peace and unity. When I wake up tomorrow, I will take pen to paper and hopefully continue to document our saga, if my dream continues. If not, I will commence on the following day after it does appear. Happy New Year, 2023.

19

Neil deGrasse Tyson

It is 8:02 A.M. on Jan 2, 2023. I've just awakened and am realizing I had a dream last night regarding the 'Train of Thought'. The wedding did not happen as planned. Yes got cold feet. Michio and Albert tried to persuade him to take his vows, but he wouldn't. Blu left the ceremony in tears and everybody else just got drunk. Except me.

All the scientists searched the entire train for the Maharishi and had no luck. Richard, however, was successful. He found Yes hiding in the Caboose's passageway to the locomotive. "Yes, what are you doing? You've come so far and suddenly you want to abandon your bride and marriage?" he asked.

Yes responds with, "How can I feel complete by marrying Blu, when the task of saving Planet Earth and its people are incomplete Richard? I wanted everything to be perfect, and it isn't. I remember telling Albert years ago, 'We cannot complete the task until the task is complete', and it's not complete. I wanted to whisk away with Blu knowing the world will be safe from itself. And how can we do that?"

"I understand sir. But remember, this entire saga involves billions of people as well," Richard said.

"I know that Richard, that is exactly why I cannot marry her yet. Those billions you speak of are as vital to the welfare of all and the planet as are Blu and I. How could I respect myself completely if I feel like I failed myself and my oath? That oath has been in place for billions of years. Our marriage will be for millions or billions more, it can wait until I've completed my work here. I must find Blu and explain it to her. I know she will understand," explained Yes.

Richard replies, "Okay, now can you help me get out of this tiny space? I'm beginning to get cramps."

Up in the locomotive the scientists have congregated.

Albert asks, "So what do we do now men?"

Silence. Max opens, "122 years and kaput."

Niels says, "Wait, this is so out of character for him, we must find him and resolve any problem there may be. The road and search have been too long and has such a great purpose."

George adds, "I agree 100 percent with Niels. Let's find the little rascal and talk."

Suddenly Yes drops down from his usual hiding perch. "Okay men I'm here, what do you want to talk about?"

Erwin jumps in the conversation and says, "Sir, can you explain what happened on the wedding night?"

Yes replies, "It's quite simple. I refuse to wed my darling without the world first being what I have struggled to have it be. We have come so far and look out there? It is worse than ever. How can Blu and I get married and leave for who knows how long knowing it is in such shambles? I'm considering breaking one of my vows it's so bad."

The group is speechless. Then the wise old sage Albert Einstein offers a solution. "How about if all of us in the group step up and call the bluff of the world's governments and show them, we are back and ready to take them on. Our history and intelligence should convince them we are for real, just by our very presence. We want our planet back. After all, what better place to make that happen than in the land of 'We the People'. Let's take a stand; make it happen and move forward in the way life was intended, peacefully and without damage to our garden of Eden and all its inhabitants. I would say, nearly seven and one-half billion people should be able to persuade 193 governments to accede. The odds are in our favor, okay? Let's give it a try. All together?"

Richard stirs in bed and his dream is interrupted. "Damn, and I was just getting to a deep part of the dream. I'll go back to sleep and see if I can resume. I wonder what woke me up?"

20

"Here I am just lying in bed, and I cannot go back to sleep. My mind just keeps going back and forth, from the beginning to the end of the story. How can we resolve this dilemma? I know I am just the writer and not the producer or the cast. The only way for me to contribute is to go back to sleep and be a part of the whole. I will continue nightly with the hopes of getting back to the dream."

It's Monday February 6, 2023, China launched a surveillance balloon over the United States last week and the U.S. was forced to shoot it down, but not until it was over the Atlantic Ocean. Russia continues to destroy the Ukraine and many of its own soldiers, for a senseless war. There was a devastating earthquake in Turkey and Syria a few days ago killing thousands. The entire Central American and South American continents are in disarray. People all over the world are dissatisfied with their governments. Immigration is disrupting many countries. People in Europe are being held hostage by Russia's control over oil and gas. The drug cartels have a strangle hold on the entire western hemisphere. Maybe going back to sleep is my best solution, for me personally. The world has changed so much, and no one is happy; I know I am not.

It's Tuesday morning February 7, 2023, I woke up to find that I hadn't reentered my dream. Tonight, the President is going to attempt to convince the population and Congress in his State of the Union address that all is well. He'll mention the economy is great, people are working, and we have no worries under his command. All lies! Afterward, I will attempt to fall back to sleep and resume my position as dreamer and writer of the nicest idea ever thought of and reenter the 'Train of Thought' with all it's wonderful inhabitants. Maybe the cast has already brought it to closure. We will see.

Just as I predicted, Joe Biden lied through his eighty-year-old teeth. Talk about exaggeration, embellishment, and entitlement. Things are going to get worse, no doubt. Who is advising him behind the scenes? China is a very large threat to U.S. sovereignty, like the simulator warned against, years ago. The wolf.

Jim Al-Khalili

Now, on Wednesday morning February 8, 2023, I woke up to find I hadn't returned to the dream again. I will spend the day dissecting Biden's lies and make some attempt to reconcile how a President can continually attempt to deceive the very constituents he was elected to serve. This country and the world are headed in a completely wrong direction and there must be a solution to halt the negative process.

It is strikingly like the content of my dreams and the quest of Yes and his scientific cohorts over the last one hundred and twenty-two years. If all of academia and the leftist governments around the world continue their efforts to confuse progress with growth, we are never going to return to our 'normal' set of ethics and values both of which are two key components to a healthy democracy. I think the key is, like Mr. Gandhi so eloquently put it, 'we must reach our children when they're young. Teach them the appropriate values of manners, trust, and truth, nonviolently.'

22

It's now Thursday February 9, 2023, as many as 21,000 dead in Syria and Turkey from the earthquake's destruction. However, some survivors are still being pulled from the wreckage. Nothing else to report on the domestic scene.

23

Mohandas Gandhi

On Friday February 10, 2023, the U.S. Airforce was forced to shoot down what the government classified as a car-sized object over U.S. airspace in northern Alaska. It was a bottle cap balloon. The information is cloudy as of today. When asked by reporters, Biden simply answered, "It was a success". Using a $400,000 missile? Nice success. What better way to divert attention away from all his lies and absenteeism.

24

It's Friday evening, it's late and time for bed. As I drift off, "Hey it's Richard."

"Richard where have you been?" Jim asks.

The group is happy to see me. "I really don't know how to answer that question, Jim. Except that I went to sleep one night, and I couldn't ever get back in touch with all of you. It made me think the story we've been involved in was just a dream. But I'm here now and happy to see you all. Is there anything new since you've seen me last? Please help me to understand things."

Back on January 3, 2023, in a booth on the 'Train of Thought' are Burt Bacharach, Paco Rabanne, Cindy Williams, Barrett Strong, Bobby Hull, David Crosby, Gina Lollobrigida, and Lisa Marie Pressley.

Burt starts the conversation by saying, "The music is the last thing I'm thinking about right now, in order of importance."

Dave Crosby responds with "Speak out, you got to speak out against the madness, you got to speak your mind, if you dare."

Cindy Williams adds, "Sometimes I light incense and a candle, it's so peaceful and quiet. The steadiness of the energy and the reliability of the warmth have a calming effect."

Barrett Strong responds with, "It was just my imagination, running away with me."

Bobby Hull offers, "All I've done all my life is just tried to better the game for our players and for those people watching."

Lisa Marie states, "I've been through so much in my life. I've seen so much. I know how fast things can change. I know someone can be here one minute and gone the next."

Gina pines in, "We are all born to die - the difference is the intensity with which we choose to live."

Paco adds, "The woman of tomorrow will be efficacious, seductive and without contest, superior to man."

All the scientists are here in the Caboose but not Yes or Blu. Richard asks the group, "Where is the bride and groom?"

Albert says, "Oh you haven't been here, have you? We haven't seen them since that terrible day ten days ago. Do you have any suggestions on where to look, Richard?"

"Is the main transport here?" Richard asks.

"Yes, it is," responds Carl.

"HMMM, sounds alarming," Richard states.

"I will go to where I located him the last time, maybe I'll get lucky." Richard climbs up into Yes' favorite hiding spot and just like he thought, here are Yes and Blu sharing some time alone.

"Hey there Yes, how are you two doing?" he asks.

Yes, and Blu are in their true biological form. He's stunned. "We are doing spectacular Rich. How are you doing? And where have you been?"

"You won't believe it sir. I think my entire experience has been a dream. I woke up when I was seven years old in 1961 and I could never get back to the story except for a few times. I'm so confused Yes."

"Confused, what do you mean?" Yes asks.

"Sir I always thought you employed me as a writer of the 'Train of Thought' expedition. Then one morning 61 years before the story was in its most present state, my mother woke me up for school, I was seven at the time. Since, I have managed to find myself back in the story a few times, but only briefly, in this present time of the year 2023. I just don't know what to think. Is it real or just a figment of my imagination? Are you real? Are all the players real? Please sir, I need your guidance."

"Calm down Richard, maybe I can help you. If you remember, early in the saga, the great Albert Einstein and Max Plank were considering the possibilities of the dilemma of the 'Train of Thought' and it's 'anomalies' possibly being in a wormhole or another dimension? Well, that may be what you are experiencing now. You see the world is comprised of many, many unknowns. I have not taken the time to explain any of these things to you during our times together because we were 'bonding' as humans like to do. We were in the moment, just like Blu and I were doing when you entered - 'bonding'.

"Think of this, if you read your books as I had you write them, you will find that all the people aboard the 'Train of Thought' were real people at the time they were on board briefly. That is not a dream. It has continued until the present time. How was it that you wrote those comments or thoughts that they spoke? That is not a dream. That's all I can explain to you at this time in your life. You have more years before you truly enter the 'Train of Thought'. Remember, I know the future. I've been there. Remember the keyhole in the Caboose. The keyhole is true. At that moment you will understand. You are back for now and that's a great thing, we were all worried for a while. Also, Michio, Neil and Jim are in the same space as you are, in their lives and in their present. Try talking to Albert or any of the others that have truly experienced the 'entry'. Maybe they can explain it somewhat better than I can."

Lisa Marie Pressley died on January 12; her photo is sitting in the lap of her father, King Elvis in the Entertainment Car.

Actress Gina Lollobrigida died on January 16; her photo is hanging in the Entertainment Car.

David Crosby of music fame died on January 18; his photo is hanging in the Musicians' Car.

Actress Cindy Williams died on January 25 and her photo hangs in the Entertainment Car.

Singer Barrett Strong died on January 29; his photo hangs in the Musicians' Car.

Athlete Bobby Hull died on January 30. His photo hangs in the Athletic Car.

Designer Paco Rabanne died on February 3 and his photo hangs in the Entrepreneur Car.

Composer Burt Bacharach died on February 8; his photo is hanging in the Musicians' Car, and all are in the 'Train of Thought'.

In the Caboose Richard speaks to all the scientists. "Men I have found Yes and Blu. They are in a state of euphoria now. I'm sure we all will see them soon. It is my pleasure to have been united with some of the greatest minds in the history of humankind - all of you. I believe I have found an answer that most of you already have experienced, except for Michio, Neil, and Jim, who have not entered that experience yet. The rest of you have experienced the passing through to the eventual 'Train of Thought', and not just in the present glorious state of the 'Train of Thought'. So, before I ask you how your trip was, can you help me to understand what I have been through?"

"Tell us what you mean Richard and of course if we can help, we will," offered Albert Einstein.

"Okay, you see, I clearly remember the entire story from the time where you, Max and Thomas Edison were on the Train sitting together and talking. That was in the year 1900. I was watching closely through all the years, of both world wars. There were many, many, other times of the human experience in the last 122 years. Seeing clearly, all the conversations between people from then until now. When Yes and Blu were about to marry, all of you were going to be in the wedding party. I saw every event for 122 years and every person passing through the 'Train of Thought'. I was the person documenting all that happened through those years, even though my age doesn't correspond with any of the timelines.

"Instantly, on November 6, 1961, I woke from the dream just before the nuptials. I was seven years old. How is that possible? I managed a few times to get back into my dream and be in the story."

"Now at age 68, soon to be 69, I'm here with all of you without explanation. I don't know if I'm scared, if I've never actually woken up, if I'm about to die, or if I have died. Please explain what you can for me, so I can understand?"

Albert Einstein opens first, "Logic will get you from A to B, imagination will take you everywhere you need for an answer."

Max Plank follows, "A new scientific truth does not triumph by convincing its opponents and making them see the light, but rather because its opponents eventually die, and a new generation grows up that is familiar with it. Patience."

Niels Bohr adds, "Everything we call real is made of things that cannot be regarded as real. Hang in there, pal, and you will see the light."

George Gamow says, "So I am just sitting and waiting, listening, and if something exciting comes, I just jump in. And you will too."

Erwin Chargaff adds, "The stress on mechanisms has given rise to one of the curses of our time: the expert. It has made body mechanics out of physicians and cell mechanics out of biologists: and if the philosopher cannot yet be called a brain mechanic, this is only a sign of his backwardness. Follow your instincts."

Carl Sagan states, "Every one of us is, in the cosmic perspective, precious. If a human disagrees with you, let him live. In a hundred billion galaxies you will not find another. And your 'Train of Thought' will take you to your destination."

Richard Feynman says, "We are trying to prove ourselves wrong as quickly as possible, because only in that way we find progress. As confusing as it may seem, stay aboard and follow the tracks that take you there."

Stephen Hawking injects, "My expectations were reduced to zero when I was twenty-one. Everything since then has been a bonus. Your light at the end of the tunnel will soon shine brightly upon your life."

"Michio, Neil and Jim, do you have anything to add to the wisdom of your peers who have passed through? Or would you prefer to enter the future 'Train of Thought' and offer your wisdom from that perspective?" Richard asks the men.

"Being here the longest of the three of us, I say we wait and experience what our peers did and come back with new-found wisdom," Michio offers."

"I agree," says Neil.

"As do I," Jim adds.

"So, what of the quest to save humankind from its inevitable demise, especially if it is as near as Yes had predicted? If that is the truth? At the present time, the evidence is mounting. No governments can handle the pressure of being in power, without dominating and lying to the people who trust in them. They lie and support their premises with a strong military backing, who by law must support the powers-that-be. Imagine the paradox of the military personal who believe in their government and nation but recognize the insincerity of the government's actions and words? It is truly the time in history where all people take a stand and speak up in peaceful demonstration so large it can't be ignored and force the powers to acquiesce to the multitude, peacefully," Richard stated. "Perhaps, I should secretly peek into the Caboose's keyhole and look at the same future Yes has spoken of. Or am I sacrificing myself?"

25

"Of all the 'Thoughts' comprised in this continuum of thoughts, the one that speaks the loudest in my mind are the words spoken by Sarah Weddington, Attorney for 'Jane Roe' in Roe v Wade: 'It is unthinkable to allow complete strangers, whether individually or collectively as state legislators or others in government, to make such personal decisions for someone else,'" Richard speaks.

"Disregarding race, gender, religious belief, political affiliation, financial status - shouldn't those words apply to all of us in every way possible? Just something for the governments and the social media powerhouses to ponder. Maybe it's those who think they know what's best for others who cause the majority of our social dilemmas?" Richard continued.

"With all the global uproar going on at this time in 2023, many valuable lessons need to be learned, soon, or all of us will be entering the 'Train of Thought' sooner than we wish or expect. After all, what lessons have we learned after thousands of years of sanctioned genocide?"

26

"I sure hope this is not a mistake. Hmmm it looks like I just slide the little door over to the right. And peek out. Should I? I want to do what's right. If saving humanity is the result of my action, I will take that chance. I will slide it, then open my eyes. Oh my God, I can't believe what I'm seeing. Yes must have been telling the truth all along."

"Richard don't move and don't shut the little portal, until I tell you to. I will be back in one second," Yes ordered.

"Okay sir."

"Okay, you can shut the portal now. Richard, you have committed a very bad thing. How long were you looking?" Yes asked.

"Barely two seconds."

"Okay, I want you to go to a hospital, now. Check yourself in. I will be there later. You may be going to the 'Train of Thought' well before your time. I don't know yet. Now move it."

27

On Monday February 13, 2023, Actress Raquel Welsh and Actor/Comedian Richard Belzer are seated in the Entertainment Car and Raquel says, "Without women to nurture in this world, how do - how do men get by? How do children get by? How does society get by at all?"

Richard Belzer adds, "That's very profound Raquel. Also, it is not impossible to succeed as a social democracy, where business and free enterprise thrive, and not abandon the disenfranchised, poor, sick and elderly."

It's Monday morning at 9:00 am on February 20, 2023. I am on a stretcher being wheeled through the local hospital's emergency room. I am being taken to a very special room designed to treat people exposed to very dangerous chemicals, or diseases. I can't speak to tell them what happened. There are some nurses tending to me and a burn specialist. I am scared out of my wits. The pain is so intense I'm amazed that I'm awake or even alive.

The specialist continues to question me. I can't respond. He says, "Sir my name is Dr. Chargaff, can you hear me? Nod if you can." After I nod to him, he says, "Sir, is there any way you can explain what gave you theses burns?" I nod side to side as if to say no. He responds, "Sir, the damages done to you are as serious as I've ever seen. Could you write a description for me, where you were and what you were doing at the time so we can prepare to treat you?" I nod my head in agreement.

The nurses leave to get supplies and a memo pad. The Doctor leans over and whispers, "Richard it's me, Yes. Hold on son, I'm going to apply some age-old remedies. If it works, please continue to act as if you can't speak."

The nurses come into the surgical room. One hands me a writing tablet. "Okay Richard try and give me some answers," the Doctor said. "Where were you when this happened?"

I write, 'I can't remember, my pain is overwhelming.'

The Doctor asks, "Do you remember what you were doing or working on when you got burned?"

I write, "I'm sorry I can't remember anything, it's all too foggy."

The Doctor talks to the nurses for a second, and orders them to keep an eye on all my vitals from another room so I have no chance of being contaminated by anything. He says to them, "I'm going to do some special research on this, I've never encountered burns like these before and I don't want to treat him generally. Keep the pain killers coming, I'll be back," and he leaves the room.

Back at the 'Train of Thought', Yes has contacted all the scientists and the Mahatma to meet in the Caboose. All twelve of them are waiting there for Yes. The rear door opens, and another Erwin Chargaff enters. He immediately switches over to Yes. "Hello men, I'm sorry to say we have a major problem today. Richard, our writer, took it upon himself to peek into the keyhole. Disaster struck and he is in a hospital in his city."

"I spoke to him directly, as myself. I acted as if I were Dr. Erwin Chargaff. M.D. Eventually the authorities will know a doctor never saw him. But it gives us time to talk and come up with a solution," Yes stated.

Carl asks, "What happened?"

"Richard attempted to peek into the future to see if he could understand it and hoped to help figure out humanities' problem and solution. He was warned as all of you were warned. I'm sorry for him being so terribly injured, I hope I can help him. Richard has been an integral part of our group. I - we all love him."

"Let this be another lesson to you men who are still alive, Michio, Neil and Jim. The force in which he was stung was extremely powerful. Another example of the power of the 'Train of Thought'. Any opinions from you men of intelligence?"

Albert asks, "Outside of an opinion, please explain what that force is?"

Yes responds, "The 'Trains' energy comes from a fuel mixture designed in my universe. You know, I do not know the mixture or combination of the fuels that make up that energy. However, the exhaust is just outside the keyway I warned about. The entire system must be shut down before any activity happens at that location. None of you have known that when you enter the Caboose. I have programmed the system to temporarily halt, and resume upon entering. Since that order had not been undertaken when Richard opened the portal, he was zapped so to speak by an extremely powerful dose of its exhaust. He was warned to 'NEVER' peek. He peeked. Now, how do we remedy this huge problem. Richard is in a hospital and questions will be asked. Any suggestions?"

Stephen asks, "Can we relocate him to the Caboose?"

"That's possible but the authorities will be searching for him," Yes said.

Michio asks, "Can anyone recognize him through the burns."

"That is extremely doubtful, as a matter of fact he may never be the same if he stays alive," Yes said.

"This is not good, we have to do something, anything," stated Max.

"Patience my friends. I was heading to the engineering section of the transport to see if I could find a remedy for this. So, stay here for a while and I'll be back, hopefully with an answer. Think of other ways we can help him while I'm gone, please."

Richard Feynman says, "During my time helping with the testing and creation of the atom bomb, there were many injuries and almost always deadly. Exposure to unknowns is usually irreparable. I'd like to see him."

Niels says, "Let's hope our friend Yes has some magic in his repertoire. We must pay Richard a visit as soon as possible."

Stephen says, "Let's all hope our friend is resilient enough to go the distance. It doesn't sound good. And I for one will feel so lousy that he, of all of us, got hurt. However, it shows you the care he has for humanity and Mother Earth."

Carl adds, "Listen, how about if we all put on our Doctor's jackets and stethoscopes and visit him together. We can pretend we are specialists in chemical burns and convince the hospital to let us inspect his damages. Since he is unrecognizable, we can burn a cadaver, and exchange it for Richard. What do you men think?"

Michio pines in and says, "I don't think Jim, Neil and I want to take part in that since we are still alive. We could jeopardize our careers doing such a wild and crazy thing."

Jim says, "I agree with Michio, count me out. It is too problematic for the three of us."

Neil agrees as well. "Yes men, we cannot partake in such an exposing event."

Yes enters the Caboose, "Men I think I have the cure. Or at least a remedy for Richard. I think the incubation chamber and the correct medical application may be the answer."

"Okay sir, we also have a solution as to how to get Richard here to the 'Train of Thought'. Let's meet at the hospital and give it a try," stated George Gamow.

On February 15, 2023, renowned actress and beauty Raquel Welsh passed away. Her photo is hanging in the Entertainment Car in the 'Train of Thought'. Just days later, on February 19, 2023, actor and comedian Richard Belzer passed away. His photo hangs in the Entertainment Car of the 'Train of Thought'.

28

Yes, Albert, Max, Niels, George, Erwin, Carl, Richard, Stephen, and the Mahatma, all dressed as doctors enter the special intensive care unit area of the hospital Richard is at. The lead Doctor serving the ICU stops them in the hallway.

"Excuse me gentlemen, can I be of some help to you?"

Erwin Chargaff, with the most biological knowledge of the group says, "Sir I am Dr. Erwin Chargaff of the Global Chemical/Biological Accidents and Trauma Center in Brussels, and we need to see and assess the patient with the serious chemical burns you have in your unit. We think the injuries may be of Alien origin. Therefore, I ask you and your staff to take extreme caution in being near the patient. We would like to take over from here, is that okay?"

One alien, one peace activist and eight scientists all with their fingers crossed behind their backs.

The doctor responds, "Yes doctors. By all means, thank you. I understand the issue and you have our word we will stay away."

The men enter the cubicle and see Richard lying there helpless. Niels Bohr goes out and tells the doctor and staff they have called for a special government trauma ambulance to take the patient to Brussels. The doctor okays the removal of the patient.

An ambulance pulls up to the rear door of the Emergency room and Richard is loaded in and taken to the local airport to make a flight, (the 'Plain of Thought'), to 'Brussels' - (the 'Train of Thought').

Upon arriving at the 'Train of Thought', Yes escorts Richard through the passageway under and over the train cars for speed. Once there he waits for assistance from No, Eh, and Huh, to hoist Richard into the incubator. He applies an emergency potion that he located in the medicinal section to Richard's face and torso.

"I hope this will do the trick to save you from damage, and possibly your life Richard," explains Yes.

A few hours later all the scientists show up in the transport. They see Richard under the protection of the Incubator. All of them have sad faces on.

Albert says, "Richard we are all here to stand behind you with great hopes for your health and your future. It was a courageous thing you tried. It shows your deep love for mankind and Mother Earth."

Michio says, "Okay men, I think this accident that happened to Richard should be the final impetus for us to get in gear and find a solution for humanity to survive."

Yes says, "I warned everyone about the power of the 'Train' and the keyhole. What you see when you look at Richard is just a tiny fraction of the damage that can occur when the next World War comes. We must prevent it at all costs."

Stephen asks Yes, "Sir how long before we know of Richard's fate?"

"According to my findings, he should be in remission already. I will keep you all apprised," answered Yes.

The scientists all head to the Caboose to talk of the future, except Stephen; he remains behind.

"Richard, I hope you can hear me, it's Stephen Hawking. Richard what you did for humanities' sake was an outstanding gesture. I am so sorry it put your life and health at such risk. I know the loneliness you're feeling right now, but trust me you have a force of great people behind you. They are all hoping for you to pull out of the pain and discomfort and come back to lead the group and the world for our cause. I'm going back to the Caboose to work on the details with all the men. See you soon."

29

Stephen, being able to walk, is back in the Caboose with the rest. Yes says to the group, "Men we must act now. You all see the graveness of the world's circumstance. We have a war going into its second year in Ukraine. All the large banking institutions are scaling down. The social media corporations are doing the same thing. There is tension everywhere. China is reaching out to Russia as a potential ally in the war against Ukraine, and certainly stocking up to overpower the U.S. someday. The scourge of the drug cartels is dehumanizing the whole western hemisphere. Citizens all over the world are lashing out at their governments. If we don't act soon our inactions will exacerbate the global issues two-fold or more. The President is clueless to the ticking time bomb. Does anyone have anything to add?"

Albert asks, "Yes, being that eight of us are here incognito, what impact, if any, do we have on this scenario, Sir?"

Yes responds, "I figured you would ask me that question one day Albert, being you. The answer is no impact, except your genius advice. Only Michio, Neil or Jim can have or do anything publicly. But we are a group committed to the ideal, correct? We need all you geniuses to devise a plan to bring the world together for once, in harmony."

"When is the first edition of the 'Train of Thought' due out?" asked Michio

"Any day now. But I believe the second book may be the most pertinent one, with regard to the greatest message," spoke Neil.

Jim responds, "Should we contact the publishing company and see if we can have them start publishing the second book?"

"Does anyone know who they are and where they are?" Michio asks.

"Good question, that's one thing I don't think we ever discussed," offered Neil.

"I will do my best to find out as much as I can," said Jim.

Meanwhile the others have come up with a strategy to start bringing the public from all countries up to speed on the need to be involved. The plan is to notify every university in the entire world. Make then understand the severity of the problems, and their possible complicity in the problem facing the entire planet and population. In the main office of the transport, the crew gets busy emailing, and faxing every known entity in the world of the plan for a global parade and moratorium, in every country and every city. Hopefully billions of citizens or more will respond.

"What date should we plan on having the awareness parade, globally?" asks Albert.

"Hold on Albert, we need to arrange many other things before we can settle on a date. Let's be a bit more patient and find out when the 'Train of Thought' book is coming out first," said Stephen.

Yes goes back to the transport to visit with Richard. Richard is in delirium laying there. "Richard are you awake?"

Stirring, Richard responds "Yes I am, who is that?"

"It's me, Yes, Richard, how are you feeling?"

"I guess I'm okay. I'm also completely disappointed in myself for doing what I did."

"Don't be Richard. The reasoning behind your action, is completely understandable," Yes told him. "I'm here now to have a long discussion with you about that and other things, so sit up and get comfortable and I'll get you a drink of water."

Richard sits up and puts a few pillows behind his head and back while Yes gets him water.

Returning, Yes says, "Richard put your hand up to your face for me. Okay I want you to slowly wipe from one side to the other. Good, tell me what you see?"

"I see everything, wow how was that possible?" Richard asked?

"It was possible because there was never anything wrong. If you remember that day, I walked up behind you and found you looking in the keyhole. Then I told you not to move. Well, the burn was placed on you by me at that time. It was never actually there. The reason I did that was because of my original order to everyone to never peek. There was never a future or an exhaust outside the keyhole. It was all fake."

"I have always needed everyone to trust me, and you took it upon yourself to take the world's weight on your shoulders alone. Maybe you don't remember what I said early on. You should, you are the author. I said, many have tried over the centuries, and look what happened to them, death. Think deeper for a second. Have I ever really needed any of you to perform the task of saving humanity? The answer is no. However, the best path was to incorporate humans, and especially intelligent, respected ones. Why? Because the damage was done by humans. Intervention by an alien serves no purpose. So where are we today? I'll tell you; we are where we were before you looked. Prepared and anxious. Perfect. Now keep this little charade completely to yourself, okay?"

"Yes sir, I will. Thank you so much."

"Albert and the rest are working their brains out to make plans to reach out to all humans. They're back in the caboose devising an appropriate way to get the message out to every pair of ears on the planet. One large problem is only three are actually left to get the message out there. Albert and the other seven are dead."

"Now you and I must discuss how we are going to explain your accident away. We need you to continue your life and continue as author, unabated. The authorities are going to be looking for you Richard. Do you have any ideas on how you can move forward in 2023?" Yes asked.

"Let me sit here in bed and take all of that in for a while. So, I'm not injured, the hospital is probably wondering where I went.

They don't know I wasn't injured. Do you know if I gave them any identification Yes?" Richard asks.

"I will be back in ten seconds," replied Yes. "There's the break we needed, it seems you had no wallet or Identification on you at the time. Success."

"Okay so we dodged a bullet." Richard said.

Yes says, "I imagine we can move forward with the plans the men are coming up with. Blu will be so happy; we can get married once the problems get solved globally. I'm going to find Blu and tell her the good news."

After a two hour walk back to the Caboose, Richard meets up with the crew. "Hello men how are you all?"

"Hey Richard, you're safe, and look at your face, you look great. The Maharishi must have worked wonders on you," said Carl.

All the men are smiling. Richard is ecstatic. "Have you guys come up with a solution yet?" asks Richard.

Michio says, "We've been working hard my friend. We will let you know as soon as it's complete."

"Okay I'm going to lay down, I'm exhausted," spoke Richard and he lays on the couch in the Caboose.

Richard Feynman sits down next to Richard and begins to express how happy he is to know the damage has been fixed. "Richard, for years when I was working on the Manhattan Project with so many astute colleagues to come up with the atom bomb, my heart was always in my stomach knowing the possibility of that war implement. We all discussed it, on a regular basis, that our work was meant for destruction. On one hand it is a great tool for creating fear in your enemy. Also, a great offensive weapon. On the other hand, if anyone else were to create the same thing, now it can be used against us, or for more sinister acts. And they have, and many countries can put it to use. This endeavor of ours is so vital to the continuation of mankind and other species. You are the key to success with the books you have written. I want to thank you sincerely as a scientist and a friend, for all your efforts………. Richard fell asleep. "Okay my friend you go ahead and sleep, you've earned it."

30

"Richard?" Snap, snap, snap, snap. "Richard, are you there?" asked Dr. Sanker. "Richard, oh my God, hello how are you?"

"Huh? Who are you?" Richard asks.

"Richard, I'm Dr. Sanker, your family physician. How are you feeling?"

"Feeling, what do you mean and where am I?" Richard asked the doctor.

"Richard, you are in St. Joseph's Hospital in Stamford Connecticut. You had a terrible accident over a year ago, and you have been in a coma. Do you know what that is?"

"I think it means a long sleep. But why?" Richard asked.

"Richard, you were sleigh riding with a friend and… Oh never mind, I will let your parents tell you all about it. The good thing is you are safe now." The doctor walks over to the hospital room door and opens it.

"Mr. Dardis, Mrs. Dardis, kids, I have someone who wants to see you. Come on in. Richard, I'll see you tomorrow, okay?"

Rushing in are four very happy relatives. "Richie, Richie's awake, yay," says his little sister Susan.

"Yeehaw, Richie's okay," says his older brother Ronnie.

His Mom and Dad reach down and all five of them embrace, in a big hug and tears. "Wait, what's going on. Where's Richard Feynman? Where's all the rest of my friends?" Richie asks.

"Richie, you had an accident at Cummings Park, sleigh riding with Martin. Don't you remember?" his dad asked.

"Remember? No, I was helping Yes, and the scientists devise a plan to save humanity. I wrote three books, and they're just about to be published."

His Mom says, "Aw, he must be dreaming still. Richie, you'll be all right."

"No mom, I'm telling you, that's happening right now."

His brother and sister are startled. "Mom, Dad, what's wrong with Richie?" Susan asks.

"Nothing dear, he's been in a coma for over a year, and he needs time to heal," answered their dad. "Why don't you two go and sit in the lobby and we will be right with you."

"Mom, I'm telling you it's real. What day is this?" Richie asks.

"It's December 6, 1962, and your accident was on November 6, 1961, the first day it snowed last year, remember? You woke up late that morning. I said your breakfast was on the table and Dad brought Ronnie and Susan to school. Then you had early dismissal because of snow. You came home and grabbed your sled and headed to the park. Martin told us you got impatient like you always do and decided to test the opposite side of the hill. It was nothing but a steep ledge and you went over. Lucky for you there were adults there."

Richard - 1962

"Mom, will you go out with Ronnie and Susan please? I want to talk to Dad alone for a while," Richie asked.

"Dad, what's going on here, we have to save the planet and all the people."

"Rich, this is very complicated. I agree with you. But how do a truck driver and his eight-year son old accomplish that? What 'Train of Thought' do we use to have people know we are in trouble? Do you know what I mean?"

Richard is so confused.

His Dad gives him a huge kiss and hug and says, "Let me go talk to the Maharishi about it and see what we can do. I'll see you tomorrow, Son." He gives Richard a wink and a smile and leaves.

31

Five minutes goes by and in the room came Yes, disguised as Elizabeth Taylor, Niels Bohr, George Gamow, Erwin Chargaff, and Carl Sagan, "Hey, you guys, thanks for coming to see me. Where are the rest of the guys. The Mahatma, Albert, Max, Stephen, Richard, Michio, Neil, and Jim?"

Elizabeth says. "Richard, The Mahatma, Albert and Max died years ago. Who are Stephen, Richard, Michio, Neil, and Jim?"

32

It's Friday, December 7, 1962 and Richard wakes up early to find Elizabeth Taylor and his dad standing at his bedside. Startled, he asks "How long have you been standing there?"

His dad says, "Good morning, Richie. Elizabeth and I met in the hallway a few minutes ago. She was coming to see a friend. She asked me if she could visit the poor little kid who was in a coma. Of course, I agreed, with her being such a celebrity and all. How are you feeling today?"

"I'm feeling good today dad. I had nightmares though. It was hard falling back to sleep. I'm still so confused about my coma. I don't remember falling over the ledge or even sleigh riding with Martin."

Elizabeth says, "Oh my dear, that's how you came to be in the coma?"

His dad replies, "My son has always jumped in with both feet forward when doing anything. We weren't surprised."

Elizabeth asks, "How long was he in the coma?"

Richie's dad says, "Just over a year, he had severe brain swelling. The doctors think he will be just fine now."

Richie asks his dad, "Dad what did you mean yesterday when you said you would talk to the Maharishi about it? How did you know about him?"

"I said what? The Maharishi? I don't remember using that term, I thought I said Doctor. I must have been preoccupied with something."

"Yesterday, Elizabeth came to visit me with Niels Bohr, George Gamow, Erwin Chargaff and Carl Sagan, dad," Richard said.

"Oh, you came to see him yesterday, also? You didn't tell me that before,

Elizabeth, why? And who are those men you were with?" his dad asked.

"Oh well, I just forgot, and the men were friends of my friend down the hall. We heard there was a little kid finally out of his coma, and we wanted to visit him to cheer him up," said Elizabeth.

His Dad says "Wait, when we were standing here before he woke up, you had plenty of time to tell me that. What's going on here?"

Richard Says, "Dad please don't get mad, they were my very good friends once before. And besides, what did you mean by talking to the Maharishi? That's what you said to me."

"Never mind that, Richie. Elizabeth, tell me the truth, what's going on?"

"Mr. Dardis, you may not believe me but, we are Richie's friends from his long, long dream while being in his coma. Just watch me," and Elizabeth changes over to Yes instantly.

Richie's Dad about falls over. "What the heck is going on here, you freak?"

Yes, walks over to the door and pulls the shade down and locks the door.

"Mr. Dardis, have a seat and let me explain. Calm down and listen. About fourteen billion years ago…."

An hour later the three are all good. Yes showed Richie's dad his powers, and a brief tour of the 'Train of Thought'. Then, the three took a brief trip to 2023.

Richie's dad, exasperated, and in awe says. "So, of all the people possible, you chose my son to be a participant and the author of three, maybe four books, about the rise and fall of the human race? How remarkable. What's next?"

"Well, what's next is waiting until the time comes when we get to 2023. All else has been done, as you can tell by the story I told you. Richard, I, we need you to try to never speak of this to anyone, ever. Do you understand?"

"Maharishi, I promise to you, and my dad, to never speak a word to anyone about our quest ever. I promise, I promise."

"Okay, I'm going to leave you two so you can talk. It was nice to meet you Mr. Dardis. I hope we meet again. See you in the future Richie," and Elizabeth leaves.

"Oh man," says Richard's dad. "I must keep that secret too. Let's do a pinky swear."

Richard spends his entire school years daydreaming of the future to the chagrin of all his teachers. His entire adult life, he is anxious for the future. His dad passed away in 1991 and never has the chance to see the results of the quest. Or does he?

33

It's Sunday, February 26, 2023. "I remember clearly what Yes said to me in the hospital in 1962. He said, 'Who are Stephen, Michio, Neil and Jim'? So, I have no idea if the dream was reality, a real dream, or a dream in a dream. It seems so aligned with all I've seen since I was a kid."

"I've done some research and Michio, Neil and Jim are all alive and doing great. I have spent many nights watching their documentaries on TV. All three represent the world of science and physics in various documentaries along with many other terrific people. Stephen Hawking was an outstanding and brilliant physicist who we all know and remember, who died on March 14, 2018. I remember thinking when he died, what a great time I had listening to him speak when I was with him and how intelligent he was."

"My first publication, the 'Train of Thought - Anomalies' is due out very shortly. I can't wait. The second one, the 'Train of Thought - Paradox', has been sent to the publisher this past week. So, in six months or so, the world will have it available to them. My third book the 'Train of Thought' 'Dreams', will be sent for publication in about three months. The task at hand now is to reach out to the world's people. But how can I do this without a crew? The world will think I'm a nut."

"I'm not fully armed with enough intelligence or an army of interested people. I will have to take some time documenting the disasters of governments for proof that there must be collusion between the powers."

34

It's now Monday, February 27, 2023. "I tossed and turned all night last night trying to come to grips with what is true. My thoughts are to go and visit Michio, Neil, and Jim where they work. Or, on the set, in the studios where they film their documentaries and hope I can see a glimpse of them, and will they recognize me? I will have to wait on that one, kind of short on money."

I went for breakfast at a local diner this morning and the oddest of odd happened. The waitress who served me had a name tag on and her name was Blu. When I came back after paying at the register to leave her a tip, she said, "Oh, thank you so much, I'm getting married in about three weeks and that will help us so much."

I said, "Oh congratulations, where are you getting married and then going for your honeymoon?"

Her response floored me. She said, "We are getting married in Negril, in Jamaica, it's so lovely there."

"I had to leave right then. As I turned away, I noticed three men in their 60's, maybe 70's, having breakfast. They looked remarkably like Michio, Neil and Jim. I was stunned again. Over three booths were four men, dwarfs, eating breakfast and talking a strange language. I started to run out. Upon getting to the exit, a man in an electric wheelchair was entering the diner. He was hunched over and had glasses on. He said, 'Hello Richard' to me. Completely shocked I ran to my truck and sat there in a cold sweat. Was I out of my mind at that moment? I think so."

"I truly don't know how to handle any of this. Everything in my life up to this day, has been an illusion, I think. I avoided getting involved with anything growing up, just so I made sure I didn't alter destiny. But then like Yes had always said, 'How do you know if you are altering destiny? Maybe what you did or are about to do is destiny.'"

"Anyway, I'm back home, cooled off from that odd experience. I'm expecting to document everything I do from here on, to avoid any mistakes. Also, If the future holds that I do end up back in the dream, I haven't missed anything for Yes' vital history book - the 'Train of Thought'."

"Reported in the news finally today, the evidence absolutely shows the Coronavirus came from a testing laboratory in Wuhan, China. In other news, Republicans are accusing Biden of compromising himself and our country on behalf of China. It's been reported that he made deals with his son Hunter and others while Vice President under Obama, with businesses in Ukraine, Russia, and China, and he's afraid the authorities in other countries will reveal his dealings. I don't doubt it".

"On another note, I'm rolling through my thoughts on the best way to get the word out about a global get-together on behalf of world peace, since it seems the dream may be over. Being that I am installing these thoughts in book four, the 'Train of Thought – The Wolves', the possibility of any immediate global effort and response is next to nothing. This book won't be available until maybe mid-2024. Unless the first two or three books raise enough eyebrows as to the real truth regarding our world. Only time will tell. The real problem for me revolves around the puppeteers behind the scenes. Who are they? What do they prove to gain by having America falter? And, what happens to me or my children, if they retaliate? The entire country is no longer a democracy. The FBI and the Justice Department are even watching Catholics and accusing them of being domestic terrorists, while the southern border is left open to any and every known group world-wide. And those groups are coming because of the intentional actions of our government. The most chilling fact is that the left-leaning news outlets are not reporting those facts. Probably for fear of the same retaliation."

35

"The signals I'm sensing is, Yes is around. He's watching me and waiting. I know it. I vividly remember all the hidden messages he gave to me during our chats, using Albert and the rest to surreally explain 'life' and 'the entry' into the other 'Train of Thought'. Is there afterlife? How did he bring back the deceased to experience the jamboree? How did he take us up to the future, which was my present, and revert us back to another present? How did he take Carl and the others back to visit Albert and Niels and Max? How did he transform himself into all those women? Is it me?"

"How could anything survive fourteen billion years? What was the other universe comprised of that would have them be so advanced? Was it time? Was it the composition of their universe? How did Yes build the train system that trailed behind to house human history? Where was the 'Train of Thought' on Earth? What was the 'Plain of Thought' actually? Why didn't the different administrations step in or step up?"

"I cannot continue this conundrum without answers. It is truly like trying to fathom our universe. Or fathom life. The complexities and unknowns are intriguing and mystifying. I'm sure many have tried long before me, men and women with far superior intellect than I."

36

Now it's Friday, February 24, 2023 at 2:27 pm. "I'm determined to stay on this quest of reemerging with Yes and the group. I'm constantly sensing a presence. I wonder if I have really fallen off the proverbial cliff or is this is how it gets in the later years? In seven days, I will be 69 years old. Am I experiencing predeath here on earth? Am I sensing Yes? Is it a dementia of some kind? I'm afraid to ask anyone my age or older if they get this way. They may qualify my insanity. Or maybe life is insane all the time."

"Wait, I just remembered the most important fact of all. I investigated the keyhole, didn't I? What did I see? Hmmm, think back. What did I see? Just a few seconds, but it was real. What was it? Yes always said it was his spot to see the future. Was he being truthful? Why did he play charades with me at the hospital, pretending for me to be terribly hurt? Was it so I wouldn't remember what I saw? What did I see?"

"Another point of aging is the memory loss. I will try my hardest to recollect that moment. It is there, somewhere in my brain. I guess I'll sleep on it."

37

"It's Saturday, I came home yesterday to find urine on my toilet seat again. I know Yes has been here. I'll look around for more clues. He's a tricky little guy, I'll give him that. Nothing looks out of sorts.

Sunday morning and I tossed and turned all night waiting for him to show, no show. I know that something is going to happen. I just can't figure out what.

Monday, I drove to the Hayden Planetarium in New York City to see if I could locate Neil. I did, and as I expected, he noticed me, watching him. But he didn't give anything away. I waited for the right moment, but he seemed to disappear on me. 'I will be back', I whispered to myself.

Tuesday, and another restless night. I had one brief dream involving Albert and Elsa having Max and Niels over for dinner, but it told me nothing that I needed.

Wednesday, we had snow for the first time this winter. Fun making snowballs like a kid. Nothing else to report.

Thursday, I woke to music playing, 'The Wedding March'. I don't own a stereo. Odd, to say the least.

Friday, March 3, my 69th birthday. "I don't feel that old, even though I've basically experienced the entire twentieth century and twenty-three years of the twenty-first century, thanks to the Maharishi. I'm off to watch a movie and go to sleep. I hope to hear from the boys soon. Wait, what's that noise outside my house. It sounds like a train. There are no trains around here. I'm going to head outside and see what's going on."

There's a huge bright light shining in my eyes. Is that? I think it is. It is. It's the 'Train of Thought'. What the f...............".

"Hello Richard. Come on aboard, Richard. We are going for a ride Richard."

I ask, "Is that you Yes?" No response. "Is that you, Yes?" No response again. Then I realize no one ever enters the 'Train of Thought' from the main transport, only the Caboose. What's going on. I say, "Yes, is that you." No response. I think, if I go all the way back to the Caboose it will take me hours, what do I do? I don't think I can scale the 'Train', it's too large.

Suddenly, standing outside the 'Train of Thought', there are hundreds of little people, all looking like Yes and Blu. I am shocked to say the least. One steps forward and says, "87g9nhmoivpj3c029utxndq9pbcy.87g9nhmoivpj3c029utxndq9pbcy0bij yv8gcw9bvumjhbng9upbxcywn4vmhvc986y3n20vm8jcn98v ph33c8045m[3pun."

Then in English he or she says, "Sorry about that. I forgot where I was for a moment. Have you seen Yes and Blu?"

I am so stupefied, I can't speak. He asks me again, "Have you seen Yes and Blu?"

I asked, "Who are you?"

He or she says, "I am Yes' father from another galaxy, these are my soldiers. Yes took Blu away a couple hundred of your years ago and we've been searching for them ever since. We finally located his transport with our transponder, and we must take them home, they're just children, and they flew away."

I ask, "How did you know my name?"

He says, "We've been watching the entire time that Yes has been playing with you people. We suspected he'd try something like this, so we had sensors mounted throughout the train. We just couldn't locate you, until recently. The universe is a large place."

"So, if you take them back, there will be no wedding? I will lose my friends too?"

"Richard there never was a wedding. They're children in our species. Yes is an exceptional being, but he exaggerates everything and has a crazy imagination. The medication he was on, he has not taken since he left, and he needs that to survive. We need you to cooperate with us. Will you?"

"I have been searching for weeks and I'm not sure what help I can be."

"Can I go inside your house for a moment, please?"

"Of course, you can. Care for a drink?"

"No thank you, Richard."

As he enters my apartment I hear, "Mpweco,vp'jm'vm5pvmjjvhcpwiv uvn5umvjmVvmpoimW4XN80NVCHCQG8CQUYG[0VCGWJM[0UF2J; 0CVMFNYHP9H0m[u54mcv09u0[."

Suddenly, Yes and Blu and Yes's father come out.

I look at Yes and ask, "So this whole exchange over one hundred and twenty-three years was a spoof, a joke, it didn't happen?"

Yes says, "Not at all, it's all real, honest, every bit. You saw, you'll see. What we did was 100 percent real, especially 2023 and the 'Train of Thought' and its passengers. The only thing I did was make up the list of scientists. Yes, they're all scientists, but I made them up to impress you, to motivate you, to get you to have humanity open their eyes to the truth. Richard, make them understand what's at stake. Tell the world, you can do it."

"So where is the 'Train of Thought' now?" I asked.

His father replies, "That my friend, you'll have to find out for yourself. Goodbye now and good luck in your search for idealism. It's rare. Now you two get on my transport and, lkleijcmv;omijvwoijmvwoimjvwoijmvoimvjoimjvwmvwmj vijvoijmr."

"Goodbye Yes and Blu, I'll always remember you. Now what? Well, back to construction, I guess. I have to stop hitting my head so much."

38

Imagine, at least ten thousand years of human history and one hundred and twenty-three years of one person documenting the 'Train of Thought' full of people leaving their words and photographs on a wall of this huge transport, ultimately finding out that the first sixty-seven years that were written, were written by me, and they happened mostly, before I was born. The next sixty-two years were also written by me, and I haven't any clue how. Well, this part is written by me but just because I've read the first two books and this one and have an impulse for continuing the saga.

As I said earlier, I apparently woke up in 1962 after being in a coma from a sled riding accident in 1961. I then spent my entire life waiting for 2023 to arrive so I could resume my quest of saving humanity and the planet Earth, In fellowship with scientists I've never met, led by an alien named Yes who claims his society caused the 'Big Bang' that set off the beginning of our universe and he'd been traveling through this universe for twelve billion years and trillions of miles before landing on Earth. How would he even know what a mile is? That is a calculation devised on Earth. Not to mention all the other questionable things.

As with all the things I pondered at the end of that supposed escapade, how did this character Yes even know of any of our travails here on earth if what his father said were true, that he had only been missing from his galaxy for two hundred of our years? I think I must go and reread my earlier books and try to extrapolate truth from fiction, so I can know my complete role in this escapade, if there is one. Or maybe I am nuts? Or in another dream?

39

Aboard the 'Train of Thought' in the athletic car is Tim McCarver who said, "Good habits are as easy to form as bad habits." He passed away on February 16, 2023. His photo hangs in the Athletic Car of the 'Train of Thought'.

Tim was seated with Ricou Browning who adds, "I get fan mail every day and lots of it from people who say "We're having a party. Could you come over and jump in the pool and scare everybody?" He passed away on February 27. His photo hangs in the Entertainment Car of the 'Train of Thought'.

Barbara Bosson says, "I swear Frank, I get more support from my pantyhose than I do from the cops in this garbage dump of a city." She passed away on February 18. Her photo hangs in the Entertainment Car of the 'Train of Thought'.

Stella Stevens adds, "I did the best I could with the tools I had and the opportunities given me." She passed away on February 17. Her photo is hung in the Entertainment Car of the 'Train of Thought'.

Musician Wayne Shorter said, "It's up to the person who's being creative to find ways to emerge and shake the world of wealth." He passed away on March 2, and his photo is hanging in the Musicians' Car of the 'Train of Thought'.

Actor Tom Sizemore said once, "I used to blame my problems on other people. But my moment of clarity, if you want to call it that, came when I was looking in the mirror one day and just burst into tears. It wasn't just that I looked bad, it was that I knew my problem was me." He passed away on March 3. His photo hangs in the Entertainment Car of the 'Train of Thought'.

Judy Heumann said, "Part of the problem is that we tend to think that equality is about treating everyone the same, when it's not." She passed away on March 4. Her photo is hung in the Activists' Car of the 'Train of Thought'.

It's now March 4, 2023 and I toss and turn, toss and turn. The recent happening with Yes made me so exhausted. Between the aftermath of the actual event and a night of no sleep, I'm just ready to head back to my bed and sleep for a week. My mind cannot put together what has really happened over all these years. Am I just a consummate dreamer or is there something real about all of this.

When I was twelve years old, my family went to a sanatorium to visit a relative who had a nervous breakdown. I was never in my life so petrified as I was that day, until now. I know there is some wild cosmic connection to the entirety of this insane drama, but I just can't reason it out.

Of course, reason and insanity are not on the same team. Why me, I ask again? Why did he ask me to participate in an unrealistic quest of saving society? Save them from what, actually? Itself? Maybe. Nuclear holocaust? Maybe. Climate change? Maybe. Disease? Maybe. Starvation? Maybe. Governments? Maybe. Or all the above? Thinking about it realistically they all are connected to each other.

I have often been accused by people that my best attributes are also my worst attributes. That statement probably applies to every person. Maybe, just maybe, that applies in a global sense. As a society, we cannot stop from self-destruction due to our over thinking and not just the changing of the wheel but, the changing of the invention of the wheel. Every idea and every invention takes commodities the Earth is running out of. Yet, we continue to push forward. Why? What's wrong with a well-tuned status quo? Excuse me someone is ringing my doorbell.

There are three men standing at my door. "Hi, can I help you?" I asked.

The man closest to me asks, "Are you Mr. Richard Dardis?"

"Of course, I am. Who are you guys?"

"Sir, we're from the US Government. Could we come in and speak to you, privately?"

"Um sure, I guess. Come on in, what's going on?"

"Before we explain anything sir, I have one question. Did you have visitors here last night?"

"Um, let me think, uh, yes. Yes I did."

"Could you tell us who they were? Please sir?"

"Well, that's kind of personal sir."

"Sir, may I call you Richard?"

"Yes of course, that's my name."

"Richard, we have a video, made by your landlord/neighbor showing a huge train coming and going in your yard last night. You have no train tracks here. How do you suppose this landlord managed to make that video tape? And keep in mind we are not accusing you of anything. We think there may be some foolish vendetta toward you by your landlord. Are you aware of any vendetta for one reason or another?"

"No not at all. They are my landlords and also my neighbors. How do you think I could have a train here with no train tracks? That's preposterous."

"Yes sir, that's what we think as well. But pictures or videos don't lie sir. Could it be they photoshopped these videos? Because there you are, right in front of the train. And you're moving your hands and mouth as if you are speaking to someone. Is that you in this video?"

"Well, it sure looks like me. So, let's go outside and check the yard for any proof."

We walk outside and there isn't a shred of disturbance on the lawn. "See now, how could a train have been here?" I asked.

He says, "Okay sir, I guess your landlord has some explaining to do. Thank you for your time and have a pleasant day sir. We may be back, sir."

I think to myself, "Holy shit, they really were here last night. What does that mean? I haven't been dreaming and I'm not crazy?" Now I know I must investigate further.

I look up and there is my neighbor shrugging his shoulders at me from a distance, as if to say what was that stuff last night. I just wave and head inside. I sigh a huge sigh of relief.

Somehow it poses more questions. Where were all the aliens in the video? How could they look remarkably like Yes and Blu? Does that transport go up and down like a helicopter? What's the truth about Yes? Was he lying and telling the truth in the same breath? Why were they in my house instead of the transport? Am I dreaming this as well? If not, what's up in the future with the G-men? And my landlord? Why did Yes' father need an army to assist him? That adds a whole new thought to this picture. Hmmm.

I will never forget that little dwarf and his sense of humor. If his dad was being truthful, I now know why he and I got along so well. Just two guys being boys.

40

It's March 5 and I woke up this morning more refreshed than lately. I guess I slept well. So many things to ponder. Writing my thoughts may help me to rationalize all that's happened. I hope. Not that it will be interesting to any readers. But they do deserve to be kept apprised of the saga of the 'Train of Thought' if there is anything left to tell or experience. I hope so and I hope not.

I decided not to go to the same diner for breakfast this morning. I don't feel the need to arouse myself in possibilities just yet. However, little signals tell me there are things still happening that show his presence. I don't know how I saw him get on that train, but I know what I'm sensing. Silly little things like the toilet seat or a spoon missing, or my blankets being messed up. He's here, I know it.

After going out for a ride for a while, I came home, and my neighbor was on my front porch peeking in my door. I asked him, "What are you doing?"

He said, "I knew you were out, and I heard a noise coming from your house, and just wanted to investigate."

I should say it's okay, he is my landlord. I rent this small house from him and his wife and they're good people. I told him, "Thank you, but I'm sure everything is okay."

He asked, "What was that huge transport doing in the yard?"

I asked him, "Were you drinking that night? Because I was just standing looking up at the night sky."

He admitted to having a few drinks, and asked me, "Well what about the video I made?"

I said to him, "Maybe you taped over an old video you took, or your wife took once."

He stammered away, in doubt. But it relieved me for a while. I went in my house and there was a strange man with his back to me, looking in my refrigerator and not noticing me being there. I slowly moved toward him. I didn't want any problems. He turned around, and it was my father. I fell back into the living room, totally astonished. "Dad, what the hell are you doing here? How are you here?"

He didn't speak for a while. He just stood there. Suddenly, I realized it wasn't my father, but who could it be? Then it occurred to me all the weird times with Yes and the changing into people. I asked, "Yes, is that you?"

And he instantly changed into himself, and said, "Hey Richard, how are you?"

"How am I? What in the world are you doing here?"

He said, "Richard, I never left. I have an ability like no other. I can be many people, different people, in many places, at many times. And by the way, that wasn't my father. That was a man from another galaxy that Blu and I visited, during our pre honeymoon. He was like an important government policing man or something. I must have broken some laws while we were there. I didn't bother to investigate before being there, their laws are much different there than here. So, we had to leave in a hurry. Blu is in your bedroom, and she looks like your mother. Don't be startled, please."

I walk into my living room, completely dumbfounded. I say to him, "Yes, I don't know what to believe anymore from you. What is the truth and what is fiction? You must come clean, now!"

He says, "Richard, how many times do I have to prove my abilities to you?

I say, "I understand all that but there are too many opposing factors now. I don't know what to believe. I must be crazy for believing any of this anymore."

Yes says, "You're not crazy Richard. This is all real. The quest, the scientists, everything. Of course, those other aliens may come back again. I snuck away just before they took off. It's easy to fool people when you are like me."

"You see what I mean? How do I know you're not fooling me right now?"

"Because I'm telling you the truth. Honestly, I am."

"You told me that you wanted me to write this saga because of my ideals, and scoundrels were the culprit and then you show me deceit. I just don't get it."

"Okay, what do I have to do to get you to have faith in me and believe in me again?"

"First, why were you and Blu dressed up like my parents?"

"So, we would not raise suspicion silly."

"What keeps those other aliens from finding you again?"

"I took off the cameras and transponders quickly from the 'Train of Thought' when we left their train. They won't find us now."

"What was it that I saw that day when I looked in the keyhole in the Caboose?"

"The end of your world, you don't remember?"

"No, I don't remember, I've been trying very hard and all I remember is seeing green."

That's correct. Earth had regrown back to the Garden of Eden after humans destroyed it for themselves. That doesn't take long you know, for nature to come back."

"When does that occur?"

"Soon."

"How soon?"

"That's up to the morons trying to kill themselves off."

"You mean, there's a variable there?"

"Of course, that's what I've been trying to tell you all these years. We are in your present now. The past is over, with not a clue to the future except what I've told you. If your people don't react soon, it's game over. For many reasons."

"Is there any reason we can't go back to another time, where we could make different decisions?"

"It's too late. The present is the destiny you've chosen. Can't change that my friend."

"What can I do Yes? Please help me."

"Exactly what I've been saying since we met. Be the leader the world needs."

"What about Michio, Neil and Jim? Can they help me?"

"No, I told you, I put them in the story for you to learn from and to support you with all you needed, intellectually. Those men cannot sacrifice their names and families. You are willing, am I correct? You proved it when you looked in the keyhole."

"What about my family? I am important to them too, aren't I?"

"Yes, but do you want your family exposed like yourself? Let's stick to Michio Neil and Jim."

"It can't hurt to ask. They were all great guys."

"Remember you have been waiting since 1962. They've never met you. Let me bring them here and let's talk to them, okay? One important thing to remember, these scientists are exactly that, scientists. They are not politicians. They are not bankers, or anything else. Originally, Albert and Max were employed because of their minds. But society has changed since then. Everyone today is a specialist. Which means the lineage of scientists incorporated to help make it right may not be the correct people to fix the problem today."

"Wait, how could Michio, Neil and Jim be in my dream in 1962 if I had never met them before?"

"Had you ever met Albert Einstein before your dream? Or Stephen Hawking?"

"Okay let's go, it can't hurt."

"Well then here you go."

Instantly, the three physicists are in my living room. Michio says, "What the heck just happened? Who are you?"

Jim asks, "Where the heck am I and who are you?"

Neil says, "Wow that was a kick in the head. Where are we, what just happened?"

"Hello men you don't know me or my friend but I'm Richard and the other guy is Yes, an alien, and we want you to help us save the world."

Neil asks, "What friend, and how did I get here?"

I look around and there is no Yes. "Well, you see guys it's a long story do you have a few hours?"

"Wait, how did we get here?" asks Michio.

Jim says, "What kind of game is this?"

I say, "Calm down men and please listen closely………………………."

After about an hour and a half, maybe more, "That's a good job Richard, I knew you could do it," spoke Yes.

"You little bugger, you disappeared on me. Men this is Yes, the alien I've just spoken to you about."

"Hi guys, sorry to traumatize you, but I needed dramatics. I needed Richard to prove he's a leader and step up."

Yes goes around shaking hands with the scientists. Michio asks, "Where are the hidden cameras, guys?"

"Sorry, no hidden cameras men. You saw how you got here. Was that crazy or what?" Yes asked.

Neil says, "Wait a minute, I smell a rat. What are you two up to? How did we get here? "

The three start to run out of the front door. 'Click' the door locks itself shut.

"How did you do that mister?" Jim asks.

"Simple, I'm everything my friend Richard told you I was. Imagine that."

"I'm sorry for the big scare gentlemen, but our crusade is apparently real again, and we desperately need your help. Will you please join up with us to help save the planet?" spoke Richard.

The trio of respected scientists are sitting in my living room and contemplating what they've just been through.

Michio speaks first. "Guys, this is almost an insurmountable task you're asking of us. We understand the depth and complexity of our world's issues. However, do you have a game plan to circumvent the powers of the world? It appears that is who you think the problem originated from and rests with now."

Yes says, "Gentlemen, we understand how powerless you must feel. Trust me, I have encountered so many in the past who felt the same way. Many who sacrificed their lives in attempts at killing the beast so to speak. But who and when is it that's going to be courageous enough to make the first and correct move to force the powers to halt their onslaught of our people and their home?"

Jim adds, "Gentlemen, we are sitting in a little rental cottage in rural Connecticut, with two unknown people, one which appears to be alien and the other an apparent carpenter and you want us to think, let alone do, the impossible, with no army, no resources and little knowledge on how to fix the world, with the weight of one hundred and ninety-three nations on our back? Count me in."

Neil states, "Well said my intellectual colleague. Count me in too."

Michio says, "Well, my career needed a new twist at my age. Count me in too. When do we start? And where's this 'Train of Thought' you speak so highly about?"

"Come on men let's go for a ride. It's just down the road in the Westchester County Airport," said Yes.

"Wait, how can this Train of yours be at an airport?" asked Jim.

"Patience, my friend, patience," said Richard.

41

Thirty minutes later the five arrive at Westchester Airport, pulling up to the hangers and there sits, the 'Plain of Thought'. They hop out of Richard's car and enter the plane, with Yes as Harrison Ford, the pilot. Instantly they are standing in the 'Train of Thought'.

Michio says, "Wow I guess you are the Maharishi like Richard told us you were."

Neil, looking somewhat pale asks, "How do you do that?"

Yes replies, "Luck is all, just luck."

Jim says, "So this is the transport huh?"

Richard answers, "No sir, this is just the Caboose. Although, Yes can commandeer the whole 'Train of Thought' from here when he chooses."

"My god, what a machine," Jim says.

"Would you like to see the rest?" asks Richard.

"We'd love to," Neil replies anxiously.

"Well, I hope you have good shoes on, it's quite a trek, but let's go," Richard said.

Yes adds, "I'll meet you guys there."

"Men, even though I think you've been here before, I want you to take a real close look at the individual cars in the train. They are all very unique and offer many interesting options and surroundings," Richard tells the others.

Two hours and thirty minutes goes by, and the scientists and I finally get to the main transport. Just as I thought, Albert, Max, Niels, George, Erwin, Carl, Richard, Stephen, and the Mahatma are all sitting and chatting over various drinks with The Maharishi.

"Hello men. I would like to reintroduce you to an unusual group of well-respected men from the past. I'm sure you all know them. Men this is Michio Kaku, Neil deGrasse Tyson, and Jim al Khalili. Presently Earth's brilliant Astro Physicists," explains Yes.

Michio says, "Oh my, are we really in the presence of such greatness all at once?"

Neil asks, "How can this be true? I think I'm in heaven. Nice to meet you all."

"Gentlemen, my life has been complete now, nice to meet you all," adds Jim.

Albert begins, "Hello men, nice to see you again, and Richard, it's great to see you again as well. I'm, we're all so glad you made it safely from the keyhole incident."

Richard thinks to himself, 'Here we go again, with the oddities of the past meeting the present, and unexplained'. "Thank you, Albert, it's so nice to see you and all of my wonderful friends from the past. Hi guys."

Michio says, "This thing is getting weirder by the minute."

Neil asks, "Please explain to me, how you men know each other again?"

"We were all part of Yes' plan to help save the planet Earth since the beginning of the twentieth century. And besides, you men were here and a big part of it all, in the later years, don't you remember?" Max questions them.

"Remember? How could we remember something we never took part in?" asked Michio

Neil adds, "Of course we are all aware of your past and your contributions to the scientific world, but I don't think we've ever been a part of this claim you are making."

Jim follows with, "Is this some kind of Hollywood joke or something?"

"It happened. I can attest to that," said Carl Sagan.

"Oh yes sirs, it happened alright," added Stephen Hawking.

"Do you have some kind of proof?" Neil asks.

Stephen says, "Just look at these photos, guys. They're of all of us, taken by my wheelchair's optics in 2022. These are proof we were all together, look. There you are Michio, Neil and Jim, along with the rest of us except Yes. His likeness never shows in any photos."

Michio gasps, "Oh my god. There we are men, all together, and the photo is dated 2022. But Stephen, you died in 2018, I went to your funeral, how are you there in the picture in 2022?"

"Very simply, an alien named Yes."

"So, what happened to our memory of this I ask?" said Jim.

Yes says, "It's just another one of those 'Train of Thought' incidents that none of us can explain. Richard is in the photo as well and he feels he stopped being in the story as of 1962."

"This is getting freaky. But we are all here and ready for the challenge, right?" Richard asks.

"Let's give it a go guys, I want my family to enjoy this wonderful place without all of the ugliness," spoke Michio.

"I agree completely. The photos have given me all the proof I need," added Neil.

"Well, count me in as well," said Jim.

"Wait, since we are all here together, let's take a ride," Yes suggests.

"Where will we be going my friend, I have to be at a seminar in three hours?" asks Neil.

"Oh no worries, this will only take an hour or less," answers Yes. "And we're off to - everywhere."

Zooming through the cosmos like a bunch of Nascar drivers at the track, all the old inductees look over at the three and they are ghost white.

Richard says, "Maybe this will jar your memories?"

A half hour later and they're back where they started. "Do you remember now," asks Yes.

"I think I've been here before," said Jim.

"Me too," adds Neil.

"Aha, you got me to remember," Michio adds.

"Have good seminar Neil," said Albert. "Hahaha."

42

It's March 6 and I don't know how I managed to get from the 'Train of Thought' to my house, but I just woke up and it's 7:30 am. I'm alone, but I still feel a presence here, like the last time. I walked throughout the house including the basement and I find nothing or no one. Well, I do have some things I need to attend to in the real world. I better get on it or suddenly the group will be needing me, and my absence may cause some issues.

On March 7 and the domestic scene, Joe Biden proposes a ridiculous amount for his 2024 budget. The Republicans have control of the house, so forget anything he tries from here on. It's lame duck time. Phew.

It's six-thirty Tuesday evening. I'm reading through the books I've written about our quest, to try and see if I've missed anything that may help me rationalize what has happened. How could I have written any of these? All of a sudden, there is a knock on my door. It's Michio, Neil and Jim. "Hello men, please come in."

"Richard, we need your assistance in solving this puzzle you've given us," stated Michio.

"Okay guys, I will try. Drinks anyone?"

"That would be nice, thank you, Richard," replied Jim.

Michio asks the others if he could start the dialogue and they agree.

"Richard, even after taking the trip to the cosmos, there are doubts. This is what we understand to be your truth. Please bear with me. Okay, what we have is a saga about an alien, who was forced to leave his original universe due to what he says was the Big Bang and the start of our universe. His parents forced this so to save his life. Along on his journey are his fiancé and three other aliens from his world sent here to assist them in their journey. This transport has an incident with some space junk and is forced to land for the first time after some 12 billion years in flight. It's here on Earth that they land. He, and he alone, discovers the damage the collision did to the transport, and he researches the ship's library for answers, finds the solution, and fixes the problem."

"Upon fixing the problem, he apparently does something wrong and causes the fuel replacement system to malfunction. While outside attempting to repair this fuel replacement system, he takes notice of the 'Garden of Eden' he landed on."

"He spends the next few billion, or so, years discovering the great place and decides to make it his new home. After witnessing all the wonders of Earth for all this time, he has the fortune of watching a new species, humans, spawn and evolve. Over millennia he watches and wonders. He discovers in short time, the new species is becoming cannibalistic and growing many other bad traits, so to speak. He watches and watches. As time goes by, he realizes the traits these humans have remind him of the information he read about in his library on the transport of his species in the other universe. And this he decides, he must monitor until the appropriate time where he can step in and repair, so the species does not self-destruct like his world did."

"Finally, at some juncture, he decides to begin documenting every person who ever lived, as a memorial for the future humans to enjoy. Or an anthropological relic for future universal travelers to experience while traveling the universe. He has posted every photo or likeness of every human who lived on the walls of this transport. Upon reaching a particular point in human history, he realizes, it's time to act before it's too late."

"In his plan to keep humans from destroying themselves, he incorporates a team of scientists and an activist from India, who he befriended as a boy of ten. It seems his plan didn't work the way he hoped, because the anomalies of the 'Train of Thought' seemed to be the paramount problem to the scientists, who apparently didn't foresee the future problems of earth by way of the Industrial Revolution's impact on society and Earth."

"Once they truly realized the problem was so out of hand, they then realized any solution was much too small to fix the problem. They reached out to various governments, who subsequently blocked any efforts to halt the problem and chose to address it sometime in the future when the problem is untenable. It appears that untenable time was about sixty years ago, hence the 'Train of Thought' Paradox.

"While this is going on, he decides to have the whole picture documented by a young boy, 'in his mind of dreams', or 'dreams of mind', the entirety of the story. The boy somehow falls off a cliff while sled riding and goes into a coma for a year. He is also part of the story, in his 'Dreams' again as an adult. He does not recollect his involvement as an adult because all he did besides work, in those years, was to anxiously wait for the year 2023 to come so he could reunite with his mentor and science buddies and complete the task of saving humanity."

"Except for some minor details I may have left out, does that synopsis sound about right, Richard?" asked Michio.

"It sounds to me, Michio, like you were reading the first books that I have written about the saga of the 'Train of Thought', Anomalies, Paradox and Dreams, which I have not yet finished. Have either of you, Neil or Jim, read them?"

"I have and I enjoyed what you have written. Although just a little elementary for me, Richard. And please don't take that as disrespect; I know you are a carpenter in life, and writing isn't your profession," answered Neil.

Jim adds, "I thought, as far as science fiction goes, there were times where I was amused, captivated, energized and confused, while reading of our trials together. The story itself is unusual for sure."

"Forget the books, guys. Can we accomplish our goal? That's why they were written. Not for journalistic acclaim, but for societies' real awareness to the impending disaster. Can you help us?"

Jim says, "Sorry pal, I went off in the wrong direction. I don't know if we can accomplish all we need to if the theory is correct."

Neil adds, "I agree with Jim. It seems like an insurmountable task, but worth taking on."

"Shouldn't we get back together with the other scientists and try to resolve this?" adds Michio.

Richard replies, "Okay, I will talk to Yes and get in touch with you men as soon as I can. Thank you so much for stopping by and talking with me, I appreciate it. Okay men have a good day."

"I don't understand this. Even after that fantastic cosmic voyage, they appear doubtful and disinterested, why?" Richard asked himself.

Suddenly I'm realizing something. Michio, Neil, and Jim are experiencing what I have been experiencing, but they don't know it like I do. There is an odd presence around. Things are not as they should be. I'll sleep on it for now. Wait, Yes spoke of answering to another being a few times in my books. But he never disclosed what or who. He played it off like it was Blu he spoke his oath to. But I never believed him. HMMMMM?

43

On March 8 at 7 am again, as usual, I tossed and turned all night. I wonder how much sleep I've lost over the years because of this quest'? Hmmm what's that noise in my living room? I better get dressed and be careful.

"Excuse me sir, but who are you and who let you in my house, my landlord?"

"Hello Richard, I'm a friend of your friend Yes. My name is Socrates. Have you ever heard of me?"

"Yes I have, you're that great writer and philosopher from the old Greek times. What are you doing here?"

"Sorry let's not confuse things, I never wrote anything. I just talked a lot. Yes asked me to pay you a visit. What seems to be the problem that he asked me to visit you about?"

"So, you've come here from the past, because Yes asked you to help me? Help me with what?"

"I'm not sure I just heard his plea. Can you tell me? Wait, are you the little boy who's writing his books for him?"

"I was a little boy then, but I'm all grown now. I'm 69 years old."

"You think so? Look in the mirror?"

"Holy crap - I'm seven years old again. What happened?"

"No, you're not. Look again."

"Come on now I'm a man of 69 again, what are you up to?"

"Okay Mister Richard, have a seat and listen. This journey started on the day I was to be executed. In short, I was accused of irreverence towards the Gods, in the eyes of the elder Athenians and they sentenced me to death. They gave me a cup of Hemlock juice to drink in the effort of making my death a suicide. What they didn't know was, the executioner with the poison was my friend Yes. Keep in mind I just turned seventy years old. He gave me grape juice and I faked my own suicide. I have to say the accolades I still get since then, are great to hear. However, I was just a man like you, trying to convince the world of their ill-gotten ways. I tried to teach the younger crowd of the detriments of government, just like you're thinking now. At that time there were a half a million people in the world, I guess. So Yes called upon me to reach out to you and counsel you. What do you think, can we have counsel?"

"Wow, that's one heck of a story. How long have you been here?"

"I've always been here. I too, like the others entered the 'Train of Thought' at the time of my eventual death. It was only a month later that I died but of my own free will, of course. The train was just a few cars long at the time. That's some machine, huh? That's how that car was named, after me and my life - The Philosophical Car. I have had to have many chats with people in the past for Yes. You're not the first. There was Jesus, John, Becket, Mohandas, Anwar, and Martin, just to name a few. You know them, right?"

"I have heard of all of them, yes. I am not of that caliber. I'm just tired of the good people of the world being bamboozled. Can you help me with that?"

"Maybe, I'll find you soon. Goodbye for now. And be careful."

"I should have expected that."

44

It's March 9, nothing of any notoriety to report except Tucker Carlson on Fox News has been showing more excerpts from the January 6, 2020, supposed insurrection of the Capital building. Of course, the Democrats in charge at the time, including Nancy Pelosi, only showed excerpts of the juicy stuff that backs up their story, helping to put people in prison, and not the whole truth. The whole truth could have exonerated some, maybe all.

Also, there is some news of late that a major lending institution in Silicon Valley may be having some serious issues. We will know more tomorrow.

Well, on March 10, the news was correct and they're talking hundreds of billions of dollars of loss and the federal government will have to step in and sort it out. Sounds like 2008 all over again. Hence, the fifteen-year cycle strikes. Coincidentally, the bank paid out big bonuses earlier in the week, to the tune of millions of dollars. So much for policing.

Socrates came to pay me a visit again tonight. It was a very enjoyable conversation. He seems like my kind of guy. But, in all he spoke I saw a mirror image of the historical facts of the past to exactly what I've seen in my life. It seems that no matter what era, or who's in charge, through millennium, corruption and power go hand in hand. As he spoke, it became clearer and clearer, that things don't really ever change. Yes has had it right all along - it's the scoundrels.

How would a simple man like me take on such a challenge of trying to create a new way of operation? The world is just way too complex. What am I missing here? The truth is being hidden by smoke and mirrors, and all for money. Or to hide the involvement of all the participants.

Maybe the future 'Train of Thought' will be a very enjoyable place to be. No currency, no lies, just people from the past with the experiences of life under their belt who can take time in the rocking chair and a box of popcorn to witness the ultimate in movies, watching people destroy themselves in the endeavor to persevere.

45

We're at March 13 and I took the weekend off from the norm of chasing Yes' dream, and my crusade of supporting Yes' dream. I think I will call on Yes to bring me to the Caboose so we can have another conversation.

"Hello Richard. I understand you want to have a talk," Yes says.

"My goodness you are always responsive, aren't you? Even until now, I'm amazed at that. I think - you appear. How do you know what I was thinking?"

"It's very easy Richard. I hear well. Unlike most. What can I do for you?"

"Thank you for asking Socrates to visit me. I like him. He was very helpful in having me understand some truths. So, what's happening with the men? Are we ready to take on the world?"

"We have been back at the Caboose waiting to hear from you."

"That's great, let's go sir," I responded.

Entering the Caboose, I see everybody, including Michio, Neil and Jim who are ready and waiting.

"Hello guys, what's on our agenda?" I ask.

Albert, as usual, takes the lead and says, "Okay Richard, we as a group have decided on how we want the plan to go. You, and you alone, are to protest in front of the White House for weeks before we come in to help you."

"What the f____," I utter.

"HAHAHAHAHAHAHAHAHAHA," the crowd roars.

"Oh, okay a bunch of funny men like Yes, huh? I'll get even with you old guys."

"No Richard you know we all care about you. You only have to do it for a week," said Stephen.

"HAHAHAHAHAHAHAHAHAHAHAHA," they roar again.

"That's two I owe you guys. So, what's with a plan, smartasses?" I asked.

"Richard, imagine, all this brain power and we're lost for a solution. Do you have any ideas?"

"Me? I'm just a carpenter. You men forced me into this. I quit, I'm out of here."

"No wait, don't leave," said Michio.

"Gotcha. HAHAHAHAHAHAHAHA, my turn."

"Seriously men, what do we do now?" asked Max.

"I have it. Let's have a wedding. There's a way to soften the load. What do you say Yes?" spoke Carl.

"You know that's not a bad idea at this point. Let me go talk to Blu and see what she thinks. But wait, I have something that is very important first. We must all go to the main transport for an important discovery."

Almost three hours later the entire group shows up at the transport as Yes had asked. "He's not here yet!" said Carl.

"Yes, I am guys, come on down," Yes spoke.

"Come on down, down where?" asks Albert.

"See the porthole in the floor? Follow that ladder down to the outside," Yes commands.

After the men get down the ladder they are, for the first time, seeing the 'Train of Thought' from the outside.

"I want you to take a look at the main purpose of my intentions, and the actual original name of the transport I had given to it over six hundred years ago, maybe more. Just look up at the front," Yes tells them.

The men all focus their eyes on the front of the train; it says one word in huge letters - AMERICA.

"Now maybe you can all completely understand my huge interest in this quest. I named it long before you were a country, after spending time among the variety of great indigenous tribes of all of the Americas. I cannot let this great place and the wonderful planet it has been a part of suffer and die. Or let it become some part of a new world order," Yes, expressed to his friends.

"So, I must ask Michio, Neil and Jim, to please drop out of the quest after the wedding. We do not want their great names and reputations to be tarnished in any way. We respect them too much for that to happen. Okay men? Richard and I will handle the rest, especially since we have nothing to lose. Are we all in agreement?" asked Yes.

Everyone nods their head in agreement.

"Of course, I will call upon all of you that have passed to assist us when we need you, and I thank you all for being an integral part of our amazing journey," said Yes.

"Now let's get the party started," said Richard.

Yes says, "I'll be back in a few seconds."

Yes returns shortly and says, "Okay, she loves the idea, let's do it. The world can wait. Let's just start where we left off the last time. We have all the tuxes and gowns and rings ready. All we need is the crowd. Okay, that's done. Let's hop on board everybody - we're going to Negril."

"Okay folks. Everybody, take your places. The ceremony is about to begin."

The Wedding March is being played by Liberace, and Captain Smith is up at the altar. Yes and the entire wedding party are poised and ready to wed. Socrates is walking Blu down the aisle and all the past passengers of the 'Train of Thought' are knee deep in Jamaica's blue waters of Negril.

Blu is greeted by Yes. They face the altar and Captain Smith. "Do you Yes, take Blu to be you lawfully wedded wife?"

"Gulp, I, I, I, I. do."

"And do you, Blu. take Yes, to be your lawfully wedded husband?"

"HRDUVIYUBKLIJGHNOMJ tryvdutfkubglih."

Yes says, "She said, yes I do."

"Richard, the rings please."

Richard hands Socrates the rings.

"Thank you, Richard. With these rings I thee wed. I now pronounce you Alien and Wife. Let the party get started. WEEHOOOOOOOOOOOOOO."

Well, I guess we'll have to save the world on another occasion.

The End of the End

The fiction is over……

And the truth begins…..

The Train of Thought
The Wolves

The saga continues as we encounter The Wolves. As you know, the Maharishi has made his mind up that only he and I are to continue with the quest of saving humanity and mother earth from the onslaught of genocide and the big war machine. So, after he and Blu returned from their honeymoon, he contacted me. I have absolutely no idea how we will accomplish our mission. In the past we had the superior intellect of some of the greatest minds in our society to help with this dilemma. I suppose we still do, being that Yes, can call upon those who were here before, and instantly.

Except for terminally ill people and people of a self-destructive mentality, I'm pretty sure no one is interested in seeing our planet or civilization cease its existence. The conundrum is not so much convincing people of the problem but, having the 'people of power' recognize the problem and solution lies with them. They probably understand more than the average person does, how they have driven us into this scenario. I'm confident their lust for power supersedes their willingness to acquiesce to a smarter, more democratic way to share power.

2

On April 15, 2023, Yes says, "Richard, I want you to take a long, hard look into your soul. I want you to take a trip with yourself into the past and presumed future. I want you to examine everything you can remember. Tell me, tell us both, what is it that you think is wrong in the present picture of society that, if you could fix, you would?"

"I would like to think for a while sir. There are just so many that come to mind immediately," Richard responded.

"Okay, take your time my friend. After all, it has been millennial that these problems have been around. Whatever it is you come up with isn't new, I can assure you of that," explained Yes.

"You know sir, I just don't know where to start. It seems that presently, there are so many pertinent issues and answers to that very question," Richard said.

"That's okay buddy. Just take your time and think, what is it that could be considered societies' biggest stumbling block?" Yes asked.

Richard replies, "Even though I am not religious, I would have to say the breaking of the Ten Commandments, is the single back breaking straw. Or the combination of all of them in one rule of law."

"That's quite an observation Rich. It sounds to me like the word scoundrel. Does that resonate with you from the past of our saga together? It is exactly the reason I started this voyage way back when. There were many times I wanted to quit and many times I wanted to make an impact. I chose, however, to wait and watch. Trust me it has caused me many sleepless nights over the years," Yes spoke.

"So how is it that we are here today together discussing a constant sociological issue that is as common to our civilization as anything else we could ever suggest? It's no different than changing shoes or going to work or eating dinner. It's there, it's obvious, and it's almost unchangeable. What can an alien and a carpenter do to fight this fight?" asked Richard.

Yes responds, "That is exactly the same response I received over thousands of years from some pretty good people as well my friend. Many of them perished because the powers that be were more willing to kill than to become decent people. Because 'power' corrupts. We see that today in the present as clear as the nose on your face. One of the alarming things has always been, and still remains, is the sycophants refusing to adhere to those commandments you spoke of. I have always been curious as to why. The only answer I have ever come up with is the fear of reprisal. I guess with you humans, fear is more powerful than truth," Yes suggested.

"So, I will ask you again, how do an alien and a carpenter fix the problem?" Rich asked.

"Through the 'Train of Thought' my friend. You see those words have much more meaning than just a simple transport from another universe. Many tyrants in your past tried to train the thoughts of their society, and most recently in the last century. Look at Lenin, Hitler, Mao, Stalin, Amin, and many more. They all fell apart. Why did they fall apart? Deception. Humans are not stupid regardless of fear. But mostly they love their families and their lives. So, they tolerate. Well, I put to you that tolerance is as pitiful as fear when it comes to tyrants. Keep in mind that religions, governments, and secret societies have always preached tolerance. In that tolerance comes followers which always leads to blind faith," Yes explained.

"Okay, so in not being tolerant we become enemies of the state. And regardless of what they preach, the state becomes tyrannical. Just look at today's America right down to the local level. Many people have died over the last seventy-five years and longer who knew too much. Even if the mission is a whole-hearted one, the tyrant attacks," Richard said.

"Correct, so use your brain, Richard. What mechanism can we use to have the tyrant make the wrong move and get exposed? We know their followers are completely blind to the truth. If they're not, they are also part of the problem. That is the very reason the tyrant invited the follower into their fold. Through coercion, false promises, and even bribery. And that started many years ago. Look at the past to determine how the present got here."

"So, everything that is happening is part of a past plan, Sir?"

"Of course it is Richard, nothing happens overnight. These tyrants we speak of have lusted for power and slowly brought forth their message of decency, as a ruse, just like Hitler and the rest. The key is to catch it early. Which is very difficult. In the case of today's tyrant, I think the exposing of the truth is in the cards already. You see, he has been flouting lies his whole life and continues that very thing today. The sycophants aren't strong enough to resist. Yet, they think they are, with their pseudo intelligence, which basically helps to conceal or postpone the future truths."

"So Yes, what can I do to be the straw that breaks the camel's back?"

"Good question Richard. Looking back on American history, it's important to recognize the length of time the original framers took to come up with a design. They could not have foreseen the complicated ways of today's society. However, in their genius, they designed a system with checks and balances. If you notice the only person elected to government that is stipulated to just two terms is the President, and that is just since the 1940's, to protect a government of people from tyranny. In this man's infinite wisdom, he is attempting to use executive actions to circumvent the system he is only supposed to administer. His games are slowly being found and will cause him serious damage and a terrible legacy. You see no person of integrity would preplan their legacy. That is only a recipe for disaster. Legacy is something that is a cause of action. And after all, who knows what their legacy is after their gone?"

"Interesting Yes, how do you know all these things?"

"A long life. Remember where I've been, my friend and the talents I have. I've been to Seminary School, Law School, Medical

School, and even have a Doctorate in Physics. So, you see it's easy for me to understand truth. Remember also, I've seen the Universe and luckily survived the catastrophic breakup of my universe. I was here when humanity began, I've been associated with the best and worst of humans. It's not hard to recognize a charlatan when I see them. So, let's get working on a solution my friend. You get thinking and I'll do the same and we can change the world, together. Okay?"

3

"Richard let's examine the true nature of the problems that are facing us in our quest. Domestically it appears that the two so-called parties are at extreme odds with each other. Politically the left wants total domination, and the right appears to want their conservative values upheld. Coincidently, both are claiming the other is ruining Democracy. How could both be possible? In time the left, because of their rights guaranteed by the Constitution, has expanded dramatically by taking advantage of those constitutionally guaranteed rights. Nothing wrong with that at its core. However, they are attempting to now circumvent the Constitution by trying to have those very rights be disavowed to the right side through claims of racism, misogyny, xenophobia, and every other avenue they can find. Quite a paradox if any. At the very least, it's gross hypocrisy. Don't you think the world powers are aware of this problem and will take full advantage of a compromised nation?"

"Also Richard, the left wants to spend as much money as possible to expand every social program they can. The right wants to curb spending, and eliminate some, in their words, wasteful spending, in order to reduce the deficit and lower taxes etc. and to ease the burden on the American taxpayer. Again, both have their logical reasoning. The question I ask myself is why such a large gap growing between the two? Has it always been this way? My guess is yes, it certainly doesn't take much to research the past in these matters. However, coincidentally, capitalism and lobbying has seemed to play a huge role over the years to the growth of the separation between the two.

Instinct tells me the main reason is corruption at its finest. It's not real hard to see the obvious."

"We spoke about this in our past books Richard. It is another example of the tyranny we have witnessed over the years. Getting back to the Constitution, the framers took a great amount of time and effort to define many things because they remembered where they came from and they wanted desperately to construct this government in ways to have appropriate backups and policies in order to protect these kind of things from happening, that have always gone on in governments and societies. And which are going on to the greatest degree, today."

"Richard, history has proven many variables that are completely relevant to this problem. The simplest example is the 'want for progress'. The complex example is in the depth of the human condition. From a psychological standpoint, what in the composition of the human mind makes up the difference in the philosophical approach to governing, from one group to the other? How does that lead to certain people thinking that playing leader to others makes them think their philosophies should dominate others political theories and agendas? I think this is at the very core of the differences between the wide range of governing policies throughout history."

"Interestingly my friend, this is also the reason why the framers added the Bill of Rights. I told you I was a doctor, a lawyer, a physicist. All true. Throughout the centuries I had plenty of free time on my hands. I took full advantage of it and received doctorates. In those studies, one of the things I found out, despite the obvious need for pursuing a degree, are the three main personality traits among all my classmates. The God syndrome in one group, the average in the next group and the people with inferiority complex in the other. Some were attempting to add to their already dominant qualities and some trying desperately to enhance an inferior personality with a doctorate degree, and some there just to earn a degree and become a professional. In any case, it can create a monster. Of course, we may never know when or why the monster gets revealed. Today's head honcho is a perfect example of one of the three, but certainly a monster. You've seen the lies he's told of himself. Ever wonder why?"

"Sir, I remember many times growing up hearing from the older people in my family that they too were worried about politicians, and how to afford things for the family, whatever. I grew up during the cold war and I remember being afraid when the city sirens would blare out for testing the system in case of invasion from the Russian military. We were all very aware even as children of the problems of war and politics. That's basically my memory of our world and the differences between the nations, and our government's philosophies. But I never remember having such an extreme indifference here at home. I know ever since the sixties and the Vietnam war we have slowly slipped into darkness."

"This is nothing Richard, yet. In all the years that you were growing up, you must have witnessed what I have globally. Always war in the world but not here in the United States for a long time, right? Well, that may change soon. The rest of the world for a long time, acted according to America's actions, suggestions or help. However, the power has shifted globally, and you can thank the money-grubbing wolves for that. So how can we make the world, and more importantly the citizens of America, recognize this impending disaster?" Yes asked.

"You know sir, it almost seems that the weakest thing about democracy is democracy itself. I'm not saying any other form of governing is better or worse. What I'm trying to say is, since everyone has a voice, it seems no one does. The most obvious to me in today's era, is that the selected officials, not the elected ones, have too much authority. It clogs up the process. We have had a government for the people and by the people, but do we? Have we ever?"

"That's quite an interesting observation Richard. You see, as I've said before, the most difficult thing for humans is to ignore the possible fruits of life that they may deem they are worthy of. Even if the fruits are not their own. It's hard to find anyone who is not tempted by success of any kind, be it materialistic or idealistic. People are fallible, what was it you said a friend told you once, 'all men wear clay shoes?' He meant ALL MEN and All WOMEN!!!!"

During the honeymoon process, along with many others, Chaim Topol (September 9, 1935 - March 8, 2023), Pat Schroeder (July 30, 1940 - March 13 2023), Lance Reddick (June 7, 1962 – March 17, 2023), Willis Reed (June 25, 1942 -March 21, 2023), Ryuichi Sakamoto (January 17, 1952 – March 28, 2023), Benjamin Ferencz (March 11, 1920 - April 7, 2023), Michael Lerner (June 22, 1941 - April 8, 2023), and Mary Quant (February 11, 1930 - April 13, 2023), have all entered and passed through the 'Train of Thought'.

Benjamin Ferencz, who was a former prosecutor at the Nuremberg trials of Nazi war criminals, says to the group "Remember take it from me, it takes courage not to get discouraged."

Mary Quant an English Designer adds, "I always say 'Risk it, go for it. Life always gives you another chance, another go at it. It's very important to take enormous risks.'"

Chaim Topol, an Israeli Actor and Painter quoted as Tevye in 'Fiddler on the Roof', "May the Lord smile with me, and may I never recover."

Pat Schroeder, a former U.S Congress woman from Colorado, said, "Government has become a machine that only runs well when gold coins are inserted."

Michael Lerner, a spirituality practitioner offers, "…In place of the old bottom- line of money and power, a new bottom-line of love and generosity is possible. People of all faiths need to shape a political and social movement that reaffirms the most generous, peace-oriented, social justice-committed, and loving truths of the spiritual heritage of the human-race."

Willis Reed, ex-professional basketball great said, "Go for the moon, if you don't get it, you'll still be heading for a star."

Ryuichi Sakamoto, a Japanese Composer offers, "I'm just delighted to be living, to be able to have a simple conversation, to feel a ray of sunlight on my skin an

d to listen to the breeze move through the leaves of the tree."

Lance Reddick, an American actor, said once, "I started to realize, a lot of times if you go into your memory, your sense memory, you know more than you think you do, from having watched and listened."

These eight wonderful professionals all passed away and photos are proudly hanging on the walls of the 'Train of Thought'.

"You know Sir, I remember almost fifty years ago when I first got into the construction business. My boss was attempting to become a developer. To all of us who worked for him, we recognized something seriously wrong. We had some clues to his troubles, but youth and ignorance are bliss. We were so-called builders. For me, the more I learned and the more responsibility I thought I had, the more delusional I became of my talents and my power. I could get on a piece of construction equipment and mow down trees with a mighty push. It made me think more of myself than I truly was. That created problems for me. All I'm saying is, even the slightest power can corrupt the mind. Of course, it took me years to recognize what I didn't see about myself then, as inconsequential as it was."

"Well then you see how all men can be corrupted by power, right? Richard, this is the message that must be brought forth to society. Even a young teenager with a gun feels exactly the way you felt back then. Remember the line you said in one of your books from the lawyer? No person should be able to dictate to anyone anything related to that person's personal life. I don't remember exactly how it was said but that is the main problem in governing anywhere. We must get this message and others too, across to everyone everywhere. But it won't be simple for sure."

"I do have some ideas on how to lessen the power of government and return it back to 'We the People'. However, it would take the entire government to agree to this simple twist of the rules. I think having every amendment or new law that is up in front of our Congress should be put up for referendum and voted on by the public. This way it would take out the lobbyist for interference and reduce corruption. Our representatives would be, by law, required to contact every constituent in their district about the new proposal, supply them with all of the facts and data available and have the public dictate which way our district congressional representative votes. This would make all of us responsible, and very possibly more educated, and will also make our representatives and senators more accountable."

"That's a great proposition Richard, as a start how do you think that would be accepted?"

"At first - terribly. But we are the reason the ideas are proposed in Congress at all. The safety and welfare of the public is the primary role of government."

"Boy you really are an idealist aren't you, Richard?"

"Yes, I am Sir. However, am I any different than the framers of our wonderful garden called America?"

"No, I guess you're not Rich, I remember those times, I was there then, and I enjoyed the back and forth of the founders for many years. The stories I could tell you."

"I can imagine. I also can imagine the difference between the real truth and the supposed stories of that era, and just like today's truths and the lies we are told. I wish people in the supporting cast would just stand up and realize the bamboozling is there to hurt them as well, and the oath they have taken is to the nation and not the leaders."

"So where should we begin Rich? How do an Alien and a carpenter begin the prophesy? Do you think a series of books is the correct path, only? Or should you finally standup and shout out to the world, your nation, all nations, your people, all people?"

"It is so complex, eight billion people, three hundred and fifty million here in America. Where to start, what to say?"

"Simple, the first step, and the truth."

"What about the martyrs of the past, won't I become dead like them?"

"Maybe, but then your ideals may die too, and before you've completed our quest. So at least trying is success. Am I correct?"

"I cannot do this alone Sir. I will need your guidance and intelligence. Remember, there are many obstacles in the way. These people, they have a workforce and a hit squad behind them."

"So do you, my friend."

"How is that? We are idealists not murderers. This is a war."

"And all wars have casualties, right? So, let's plan and the 'Train of Thought' will be your army. Start explaining yourself to the multitude and make them see the truth. And maybe the casualty will be the corruption itself."

"Sir you can open the internet any time of the day and see people everywhere espousing the same talk and ideals. It is just listened to and not heard or acted upon and it's time act and to be heard."

"I don't agree with you Richard. Those very people doing the talking will join in two seconds, then you have an army. However, we must be careful on how we word our intentions. Example, the word army could be mistaken for anarchy or a violent group. We must classify it as peaceful presentation of unanimous consent. We don't want violence and destruction; we want peaceful understanding and non-violence. But we want our government to accede to our considerations and desires of 'We the People'."

"So, I ask you again sir, how are we supposed to use this 'Train of Thought' as the conduit to social adherence and awareness, without the appearance of another brainwashing."

"I would suggest that you use your fictional books and any other paraphernalia to offer an opening of togetherness and commonality to have government see your messages and desires and offer the public an open forum of communication and conversations of truth and cohesiveness between your government and their constituency, like social media. It may just be the impetus the country needs to force the supposed royalty to acquiesce to a better present and future. It's worth a try, isn't it?"

"Yes, I suppose it is. Of course, the deep state will pounce like a tiger, won't it?"

"Isn't that what we want? As proof of their involvement in the existing problem. Who's to say that they aren't the main problem globally in the first place? After all, that has been the silent warning hovering for years anyway. Why do you think so many other countries have put a target on the back of America for so long? The contender always wants the champion to fall and fall hard."

"Of course, that's what we want but we mostly want America not to fall. We want America to rise back up, but honestly and humanely. I think trying to reach out to the conscience of all Americans, young and old, rich or poor, Republican or Democrat, Black, White, Asian, Latino, Indigenous and every other denomination that we are one family, who simply want honesty, integrity, and peace, for all involved. We want our country back."

Entering the 'Train of Thought' recently, and sitting together chatting are Lenny Goodman (April 25, 1944 - April 22, 2023), Harry Belafonte (April 25, 1927 – April 25, 2023), Jerry Springer, (February 13, 1944 - April 27, 2023), Gordon Lightfoot (November 17, 1938 – May 1, 2023), Tory Bowie (August 27, 1990 - May 2, 2023), Vida Blue (July 28, 1949 - May 6, 2023), Jim Brown (February 17, 1936 -May 18, 2023), Tina Turner, (November 26, 1939 - May 24, 2023).

Lenny Goodman, a renowned British ballroom dancer and dancing judge once said, 'Watching you was like watching a stork who had just been struck by lightning'.

Harry Belafonte, an American singer-actor responded, 'One of the true pleasures of my life has been the work of John Steinbeck. He was one of the people who turned my life around. I had no direct relationship with him, unfortunately.'

Jerry Springer, an American broadcaster-journalist said, 'I think technology has changed the way we see things. Human behavior has not changed in 3000 years. There's nothing that has ever been on our show that isn't in the Bible that isn't in literature, that isn't in Shakespeare.'

Gordon Lightfoot, the Canadian singer, writer, and performer adds, 'Let our hearts touch far horizons. Let our love know no borders. Draw the circles wide until, no one stands alone.'

Torie Bowie, an American track and field athlete, said, "One day I hope that I can come to Sandhill, and there's a huge sign that says, 'Welcome to Sandhill home to Torie Bowie'."

Vida Blue, an Oakland Athletics superstar, said, 'It's a weird scene. You win a few baseball games and all of a sudden, you're surrounded by reporters and TV men with cameras asking you about Vietnam and race relations.'

Jim Brown, professional football all-time great once offered, 'Education, family, character, intelligence, humility, okay? These are the things that make culture live.'

Tina Turner, American singer-performer, offers, 'You take your problems to a God, but what you really need is the God to take you to the inside of you.'

All these heroes entered and passed on the 'Train of Thought' along with countless others.

Having agreed to meet today, May 25, 2023, in the Caboose of the 'Train of Thought', Richard enters to find all of his old cronies on board and chit-chatting about their lives in the other places they have been, probably many different locations. The first to offer a big hello is Albert. Then, one by one they all greet Richard.

"I have been waiting for this time, I'm happy to see all of you," Richard spoke.

"Oh, I see you all have shown up as I requested," spouts Yes.

However, missing are Michio, Neil and Jim. Yes does not want those great men to jeopardize their lives and careers while they are still living.

"Okay men. Richard and I have been talking and we want any input from all of you pertaining to the global issues you all remember that are confronting us at this time."

"Wait, how was your honeymoon with Blu?" asks Carl.

"Oh, thanks for asking Carl. It was fantastic."

"Should we all expect to be called uncle someday, Yes?" asked Max Plank.

"Not anytime soon my friends, we want to enjoy our lives alone and together for now. But thanks for the suggestion. So do any of you have any ideas?" Yes asked.

Stephen Hawking says, "I've been thinking quite a lot about this, and I have the perfect plan. Please don't react to my plan yet until

I've completely laid it out, okay gents? It is not too difficult. The first thing is we must blend in with the so- called deep state. That's who is doing all the covering up, and they're paid well to accomplish the goals of the people of power. So, we must infiltrate them quietly and expose them in overt ways. You see that the Congress is presently working to expose the wolves, but they may need help."

George Gamow says, "Lay it on us buddy, we are all ears."

Socrates adds, "I admire your intellect sir, please enlighten us."

"Okay, since we have all agreed that you can't change destiny that hasn't happened yet then, let's do just that. What I mean is, since all of us are dead, except Richard, we can be recreated instantly by our wonderful host into present day Paul Reveres. Remember, the British are Coming, the British are Coming. Well, I think we divide the US into eleven different regions. Each one of us takes a region and we sell the 'Train of Thought' philosophy to as many people that will hear us as we can. Spreading the word of cohesiveness, continuity, honesty and above all anti- corruption. We will first show the country the example of the present-day tyrant and his families' extensive background of lies and global corruption. Then we will provide them the opportunity to follow us into the next election with a coherent strategy that will retake America's position in the international community only with honesty and integrity."

"From there we will drop a NEW BOMB, of truth, justice and the American way to the rest of the world's population. Everything I see in the world is no different than here at home. The people want to be free of the dirt, free of the corrupt, free of poverty and they want humane living conditions. We can achieve all those things."

Niels speaks, "Of course, I am not American, but I do understand from what I've seen, America's influence on the world has seriously been depleted. I think we all know why. Stephen, your plan sounds like it can work. However, we must make sure somehow that the typical scoundrels don't try their usual charlatan approach and weasel their way back into the fold. We must absolutely prevent the past from reoccurring. I think the good men and women in government could rewrite the laws to inject those variables into the Bill of Rights and make it impossible to return to today's times again."

Erwin Chargaff offers, "I am in complete agreement with the idea. We are all scientific men with great backgrounds. I see no reason we cannot develop the appropriate moniker for our crusade. It should include the 'Train of Thought' message along with the use of the principles we all carried through our personal lives. After all, we're all passed, aren't we. At least I think we are. Hahahaha."

The Mahatma says, "I like the Idea, but absolutely no subterfuge, please. I will not tolerate any bad behavior. Bad behavior is too easy to return to. Especially since we can't be charged for doing anything wrong because we don't exist."

"Always the Idealist Mohandas, huh? How idealistic are the scoundrels when they have people killed? Like John Kennedy, Hale Boggs, Vince Foster and possibly Ron Brown and Antonin Scalia, just to name a few. These people we are thinking of challenging are as ruthless as Hitler, Stalin, and any other notoriously bad tyrant. Richard, you are the only one of us that can be harmed so watch your back," Albert Einstein stated.

Richard Feynman adds, "It sure is apparent from the last decade or more that the world has become a different place. If we do not act on this now the next war will be our last war. I for one, would hate to see from my new place of existence no world to look down upon any longer. Besides the destruction could very well destroy us as well."

Carl Sagan asks, "So what exactly is the 'Train of Thought' message we are sending? Let's make that clear at the front."

Richard says, "If you all read the first three books, you will see that everyone who came aboard were accented and accepted as equal. Women, Indigenous people, non-Americans, all peoples of color, educated people, uneducated people. The only persons that were subject to any scrutiny were bad people of the past. They were left to freeze for the public to view because of their dirty deeds. The very premise of who we need to have to change or combat legally."

Boarding the 'Train of Thought' are Jacky Oh (May 3, 1990 - May 31, 2023), Jim Hines (September 10, 1946 - June 3, 2023), Astrud Gilberto (May 29, 1940 - June 5, 2023), Francoise Gilot (September 26, 1921 - June 6, 2023), Roger Payne (January 29, 1935 - June 10, 2023), Treat Williams (December 1, 1951 - June 12, 2023), Cormac McCarthy (July 20, 1933 - June 13, 2023).

Jacky Oh, an American performer, suggests to the others, "When you start drawing nearer to God, reading and really listening to the word and applying it in real life - there's such a beautiful awakening and transforming power that you start to feel & I just really love that for me and also for my loved ones that are experiencing that as well. Every conversation that I've had lately has God all up in it & he really has the answer to every single thing."

Jim Hines, an American Sprinter who first broke the 10 second mark in the 100 meters said, "A couple of us spoke about our connection to each other and how important basketball was to us as young kids, and we encouraged kids out there to embrace this time."

Astrud Gilberto, a Brazilian singer quoted, "When our enemies shut a door, God opens a window."

Francoise Gilot, a French Artist stated once, "…Since I realized that Picasso lived in a self-enclosed world and that his solitude was therefore total, I wanted to explore my own solitude."

Roger Payne, an American biologist spoke, "Whales and redwoods both make us feel small and I think that's an important experience for humans to have at the hand of nature. We need to recognize that we are not the stars of the show. We're just another pretty face, just one species among millions."

Treat Williams, an American actor who starred in the movie 'Hair" has said, "I define success as being comfortable with yourself and your life. And that is about as good as it gets, really."

Cormac McCarthy, an American Novelist and Playwright wrote once, 'When the lamb is lost in the mountain, he said. They is cry. Sometime come the mother. Sometime come the wolf.'" Apropos for this time in our lives.

All those fine professionals have entered and passed through the 'Train of Thought' and their photos hang elegantly on the walls.

"We need an express lane to the population. So, let's get hopping men," spoke Mohandas.

"I'm going to go get millions of tee shirts made up. The 'Train of Thought' on the back and front," spoke Richard.

"Great idea pal. I will diagram the fourteen regions we need to emphasize in the country and give each one of us those locations. In this time of technology, we will all have cellphones with sixteen of the others programmed in each, okay?" said Yes.

"I would like to stay in contact with Michio, Neil, and Jim if we could. Remember, they put in a ton of effort in the past. And great guys too," said Carl.

"Yes, that's a great idea Carl, they became dear friends of ours too. But we cannot expose any activity they may do. Also Yes, why do we need sixteen cell phones?" asked Stephen.

"Okay, I was wondering when someone would ask that question. Men, I have one more surprise to lay on you. I don't know why I never thought of this in the past," said Yes, as he opens the caboose door to the last car, which happens to be named the Integrity Car. "I want you all to meet and accept Dr. Martin Luther King Jr. to our team. Martin, please say hello to all of our contributors."

"Hello everyone, I hope you all remember me! I certainly remember all of you. Except of course you much younger men. I'm happy to come aboard. Yes has explained everything about your crusade and I am in complete agreement, and anxious to help," expressed Martin.

All the men applaud Martin and separately introduce themselves one at a time.

Martin offers, "I too have been watching the world slowly sink into it's present despair from my place of retirement. It sure is amazing what you can find out about your supposed friends and enemies when you're perched above and finding out the truth. So let us get on with the appropriate awareness campaign."

"Nicely put Sir, we all respect your past and are excited to have you on board. You will make a great teammate," Richard offered.

"Okay men, on these sheets of paper I'm giving you are the sixteen regions of the country that I have decided that each of you should concentrate on. Each of you, please take an area and go to work. You can take any identity you wish. Remember you cannot be arrested or attacked. I have used my powers to shield you all from harm and scrutiny except Richard, our author," spoke Yes.

"Before you all embark on the greatest international attempt to unite the country and the world on the absolute unification of the single most important event of our world, I want to petition each of you to offer one last statement to the readers of our quest, of your heartfelt opinion on this subject. Please, and let's start with you Socrates," asked Yes.

"Thank you Yes, my friend. 'I tell you that wealth does not make a good within, but that from inner goodness comes wealth and every other benefit to man. This is my teaching, and if it corrupts youth, then I suppose I am their corruptor. Well, my fellow Americans, you must now decide to acquit me or not. Just as I quoted to the Athenians all those years ago. Thank you."

"Thank you, Socrates. Mohandas next please," spoke Yes.

"Thank you Yes. One fasts for health's sake under laws governing health, fasts as a penance for a wrong done and felt as such. In these fasts, the fasting one need not believe in Ahimsa. Here is, however, a fast which is votary of non-violence sometimes feels impelled to undertake by way of protest against some wrong done by society, and this he does when as a votary of Ahimsa has no other remedy left. Such an occasion has come my way, again as in nineteen hundred and forty-eight, when I first spoke these very words. Thank you."

"Thank you, Mohandas, Albert Einstein please," Yes asked.

"Where the world ceases to be the scene of our personal hopes and wishes, where we face it as free beings admiring, asking, observing, there we enter the realm of art and science. And although I am a typical loner in daily life, my consciousness of belonging to the invisible community of those who strive for truth, beauty and justice has preserved me from feeling isolated. Learn from yesterday, live for today, hope for tomorrow, the important thing is to not stop questioning. These three were different quotes during different days of my life and put together as a signal to today's common man. Thank you."

"Thank you, Albert. Max Plank, please."

"Thank you Yes. When I look back to the time, already one hundred and twenty-three years ago, the concept and magnitude of the physical quantum of action of the 'Train of Thought' for the first time, to unfold from the mass of experiential facts, and again, to the long and ever torturous path which led, finally, to it's disclosure, the whole development seems to me to provide a fresh illustration of the long since proved saying of Goethe's that man errs as long as he strives. And the whole strenuous intellectual work of an industrious research worker would appear, after all, in vain and hopeless, if he were not occasionally, through some striking facts, to find that he had, at the end of all his crisscross journeys, at least accomplished at least one step which was nearer the truth. An indispensable hypothesis, even though still far from being a guarantee of success, is however the pursuit of a specific aim, whose lighted beacon, even by initial failures, is not betrayed. I have indulged myself the need to alter an original quote of mine here today for the purpose of our quest. Thank you."

"Very good Max. And Niels Bohr."

"Thank you Yes. I will steal lines from my Nobel acceptance speech here today. In attempting to give expression to my heartfelt gratitude for the great honor that the Maharishi has bestowed upon me by awarding me the opportunity to partake in his quest all those years ago, I am naturally forcibly reminded of Albert Nobel's insistence upon the international character of science, which indeed forms the very basis of his munificent bequest. That point of view - the international character of science - suggests itself all the more readily to myself, as the contributions that I may have had the good fortune to make to the development of this quest of ours, consist of a combination of all our deep intellect and commitment to our mother earth and all her inhabitants."

"Thank you, Niels. Please George Gamow."

"Thank you, Yes. I will repeat again and again, it took less than an hour to make the atom, a few hundred million years to create the planets but five billion years to create man. And the supposed intellects of government, are intent on destroying all of us through politics and power and cannot recognize their myopia through their own large egos. We desperately need to advance through diplomacy, not indifference of ideology. Thank you."

"Thank you, George. Next Erwin Chargaff, please."

"Thank you, Yes. One of the most insidious and nefarious properties of the scientific models is their tendency to take over, and sometimes supplant, reality. Well, that very proposal is happening in governments today and probably always has. The very idea of espousing views that are singular to one's own opinion on the multitude is always recipe for failure. That is not Democracy. That is Tyranny. And we must stop it everywhere it is blossoming. And it is blossoming everywhere. Thank you."

"Thank you, Erwin. Next please Carl Sagan"

"Thank you Yes. I will employ a variety of past statements of mine to make a more complete observation of our dilemma today. We live in a society exquisitely dependent on science and technology, in which hardly anyone knows about science and technology. Science is a way of thinking much more than it is a body of knowledge. For me it is far better to grasp the universe as it is really than to persist in delusion, however satisfying and reassuring. That, in itself, also lends to the slow burn of power and corruption during our growth as a nation. Somewhere, something incredible is waiting to be known. For small creatures such as we, the vastness is bearable only through love. One thing I've taken notice of from my perch where I reside now is, the bamboozle continues greater than ever before. You must as a society of commonality persevere. To do so is to take your place in history and put an end to the tyranny disguised as democracy, now through the 'Train of Thought', thank you."

"Thank you, Carl, next please Richard Feynman."

"Thank you, Sir. As I've said in the past, I would rather have questions that can't be answered than answers that can't be questioned. In this moment in history, it seems our President won't answer any questions. This is unacceptable and highly questionable. It doesn't matter how beautiful his theory is, it doesn't matter how smart he thinks he is. If it doesn't agree with experiment, it's wrong, and he/they are wrong. When they reach the 'Train of Thought' and pass on, they will see what we are all espousing here today. Thank you for listening to my words."

"Thank you, Richard. Next please Stephen Hawking."

"Thank you, Sir. As I've said before, "Life would be tragic if it weren't funny. Many people find the universe confusing—it's not. People who boast about their IQs are losers. Have you heard that our president brags about his IQ? Also black holes ain't as black as they are painted. They are not the eternal prisons they were once thought. Things can get out of a black hole both on the outside and possibly to another universe. So, if you feel you are in a black hole, don't give up- there's a way out. Most of the threats we face come from the progress we've made in science and technology. We are not going to stop making progress, or reverse it, so we must recognize the dangers and control them. Just like the dangers we face from our deep state and governments. I'm an optimist and I believe we can succeed through the 'Train of Thought'. Thank you."

"Thank you, Stephen, and our new inductee Dr. Martin Luther King."

"Thank you, Sir. First, I want to thank you for the great invitation into this illustrious forum of so many intelligent and worldly scholars. To be involved in this quest is not only my sincerest, but humblest responsibility. Let me say, as my friends before me, I will use many of my past quotes together to sum up my opinion of what is obvious to me from beyond. 'Love is the greatest force in the universe. It is the heartbeat of the moral cosmos. He who loves is a participant in the being of God.' 'True peace is not merely the absence of tension; it is the presence of justice.' 'If you can't fly, then run; if you can't run, then walk; if you can't walk, then crawl; but whatever you do. you have to keep moving forward.' 'The ultimate measure of a man is not where he stands in moments of convenience and comfort, but where he stands in times of challenge and controversy.' The present-day heads of state are not standing so well in times of challenge and controversy. It is now that the common man, more than ever before, must rise together and challenge the hegemonic state from destroying humanity, and that is no more obvious than in the present-day White House and all other world capitals. Thank you."

"Thank you, Martin. And now our Author and friend Richard Dardis."

"Thank you, Yes. And thanks to all of you highly intellectual men who have taken me into your lives and hearts. Of course, this 'Train of Thought' crusade was my personal dream. However, no man could accomplish such an idealistic pursuit as this without having been a dreamer in the first place. It has been a painful search over these many years to attempt to locate, in my mind, a place that is idealistic, iconic and without fear and prejudice. I am aware that I too have taken part in those very properties myself on occasion. However, it does not take anyone of the deep and cosmic senses of all of you fine people to recognize the sincerity of the average person seeking to qualify their very own set of dreams and successes, only to have the weight of overpowering governments upon one's neck and shoulders. The premise to which we use to stand up to and pledge has dissipated into power and money and lies and coverup. Again, it does not take deep intellect to see the truth. Only open eyes. For far too long, our eyes were kept shut due to our own desires of accomplishment and dreams. However, those dreams have slowly been shattered by the perpetuating darkness of hegemonic greed. In this dialogue of a saga relating to the past industrial, technological, militaristically weaponization of our societies. We are no longer free to dream the dream. We are subservient to government instead of the opposite. That needs to be reversed immediately. I implore all who read these letters and words to take part in a global exercise of determination and awareness. Thank you"

"Thank you, Richard and thanks to all of you for your well said dissertations. Now, it's my turn. I was fortunate to stumble upon this garden a long time ago. There is no better place in the universe, I promise you that. Once we destroy this haven, we have nowhere else to go that is reachable. The next option is to find balance for all who are here now. That cannot happen with corrupt governments and people. The most egregious example is what has gone on in the USA since the beginning of the industrial revolution. Not solely because of the ecological destruction either. With all the growth, imagine how much has been stolen or corrupted. It is unfathomable that a vice president could sell his country away to other countries, for the purpose of greed when the money cannot possibly legitimately be spent - ever. Or by himself at all. But he did that very thing and under the watchful eyes of equal or blind participants. It is exactly like the robber barons of the past. Of all the past delinquencies our country is guilty of, if this one is not prosecuted, we will fail and won't ever be a beacon or guiding light of freedom and prosperity again. The wrong-doings of this administration are unlimited. Onward with the battle men," spoke Yes.

My deepest thanks to my cast of characters, which includes in order of appearance:

Albert Einstein, Max Planck, Niels Bohr, George Gamow, Erwin Chargaff, Carl Sagan, Richard Feynman, Stephen Hawking, Michio Kaku, Neil deGrasse Tyson, Jim Al-Khalili, Mohandas K. Gandhi and Socrates.

Also, my sincerest respects and thanks to all the characters who passed through the 'Train of Thought' Anomalies. By order of appearance:

Richard Trevithick, Thomas Edison, Teddy Roosevelt, Franklin Roosevelt, Harry Truman, Benjamin Harrison, William McKinley, Marie Curie, Sigmund Freud, Nickola Tesla, Ivan Pavlov, Alexander Fleming, Robert Goddard, Edwin Hubble, Levi Strauss, Walter Reed, Cy Young, Ty Cobb, Julia Grant, Dwight Eisenhower, Pope Leo XXIII, Susan B Anthony, Paul Gaugin, Mark Twain, Leo Tolstoy, Calamity Jane, Harriet Tubman, Antonin Dvorak, Scott Joplin, Jules Verne, Anton Chekov, Herbert von Bismarck, Chief Joseph, Joseph Pulitzer,, Paul Cezanne, Sarah Goode, James Agee, Virgil Earp, Florence Nightingale, John Astor, J.P. Morgan, Jack London, Edgar Degas, Grover Cleveland, Butch Cassidy, Sundance Kid, Etta, Pat Garrett, Billy the Kid, George Westinghouse, Rudolf Diesel, Geronimo, Red Cloud, Mary McKillop, Clara Barton, Alexander G. Bell, William Porter, Gustav Maher, Booker T. Washington, Bram Stoker, Buffalo Bill Cody, Grigori Rasputin, Tsar Nicholas II, Captain Edward Smith, Archduke Ferdinand, Mata Hari, Alois Alzheimer, Claude Debussy, Bat Masterson, Andrew Carnegie, Pierre Renoir, Manfred von Richthofen, Henry Ford, Harvey Firestone, Harry Houdini, Pancho Villa, Warren Harding, Sarah Bernhardt, Nellie Bly, William Jennings Bryan, Calvin Coolidge, Ernest Shackleton, Claude Monet, Gustav Eiffel, Franz Kafka, Woodrow Wilson, Bessie Coleman, Annie Oakley, Christy Matthewson, Rudolf Valentino, Vladimir Lenin, Sun Yet-Sen, Lizzie Borden, Babe Ruth, Lou Gehrig, Arnold Rothstein, John Dillinger, Al Capone, George baby faced Nelson, Charles pretty boy Floyd, William Taft, Wyatt Earp, Kahlil Gibran, John P. Sousa, Ida B Wells, Isadora Duncan, Karl Benz, George Eastman, Fatty Arbuckle,

Thomas Hardy, Plato, D.H. Lawrence, Arthur Conan Doyle, Lon Chaney, Knute Rockne, Bonnie Parker, Clyde Barrow, Mollie Brown, Annie Bessant, Amelia Earhart, Clarence Darrow, Dutch Schultz, Ma Barker, Fred Barker, Will Rogers, Typhoid Mary Mallon, Elsa Einstein, Huey Long, Rudyard Kipling, John D Rockefeller, James Joyce, Virginia Woolf, W.B Yeats, Jean Harlow, Robert Wadlow, George Gershwin, Jack Johnson, Walter Johnson, James Naismith, Marcus Garvey, Carole Lombard, John Barrymore, Beatrix Potter, George Patton, George M. Cohan, Gertrude Stein, Black Dahlia Elizabeth Short, Glenn Miller, Franz Boas, H.G. Wells, Erwin Rommel, Benito Mussolini, W.C. Fields, Henry Ford, Hideki Tojo, Adolf Hitler, Orville Wright, Charles Ponzi, Margaret Mitchell, George B. Shaw, Anne Frank, Douglas McArthur, Michelle, Paul, Lucy, John, Mary, Lucille, Lil Richie, Donna, Sam, Mary, Mandy, Toto, Lassie, Marley,, Scoobey Doo, Ben, Buddy, Elton, Daniel, Maybelline, Suzie, George Orwell, Edgar Rice Burroughs, Al Jolson, William Hearst, Curly Howard, Jim Thorpe, Henri Matisse, Joe Jackson, Mick Jaggar, Keith Richards, Bob Dylan, Joan Baez, Dennis Wilson, Brian Wilson, Jim Morrison, Robbie Krieger, Janis Joplin, John F Kennedy, Robert Kennedy, Evita Peron, Eliot Ness, J.E. Hoover, Jimi Hendrix, Enrico Fermi, Dylan Thomas, Malcolm X, Otis Redding, Robert Frost, Mahalia Jackson, Hattie McDaniel, Hank Williams, Alan Turing, Frank Sinatra, Tony Bennett, John Lennon, Elvis Pressley, Charlie Parker, Emmitt Till, A.A. Milne, Bela Lugosi, Jackson Pollock, Tommy Dorsey, Babe Zaharias, Laura Wilder, Humphrey Bogart, Oliver Hardy, Christian Dior, Rosalind Franklin, Pope Pius XII, Tyrone Power, Fidel Castro, Richie Valens, Buddy Holly, Big Bopper, Lou Costello, George Reeves, Billy Holiday, Errol Flynn, Richard Wright, Zora Neale Hurston, Clark Gable, Ward Bond, Ernest Hemingway, Carl Jung, William Faulkner, Gary Cooper, Marilyn Monroe, Roger Maris, Ham the Chimp, Lucky Luciano, Pope John Paul XXIII, Medgar Evers, W.E.B. Dubois, Jawaharlal Nehru, Ian Fleming, Sam Cooke, Winston Churchill, Albert Sweitzer, Dorothy Dandridge, Nat King Cole, T.S. Eliot, Walt Disney, Elizabeth Taylor, Vivian Leigh, Hellen Keller, Montgomery Clift, Lenny Bruce, Margaret Sanger,

Mama Cass Elliot, Gus Grissom, Ed White, Rodger Chafee, Robert Oppenheimer, Spencer Tracey, Dr. Martin Luther King, Ho Chi Minh, John Steinbeck, Maria Callas, Neil Armstrong, Buzz Aldrin, Rocky Marciano. These ladies and Gentlemen were all proudly displayed in book one the 'Train of Thought', Anomalies.

Thank you and respect to all the characters in book two, the 'Train of Thought' Paradox. By order of appearance:

Jimi Hendrix, Janis Joplin, Tammi Terrell, Jim Morrison, Duane Alman, Louis Armstrong, Bertrand Russel, Kris Kristofferson, Vince Lombardi, Audie Murphy, Nikita Khrushchev, Josephine Baker, Coco Chanel, Jackie Robinson, Mahalia Jackson, Dan Blocker, Roberta Flack, Don Mclean, Roberto Clemente, Richard Nixon, Henry Kissinger, Pablo Picasso, Bruce Lee, J.R. Tolkien, Jim Croce, Bobby Darin, Rod Serling, Oskar Schindler, Charles Lindbergh, Walter Brennen, Buford Pusser, Duke Ellington, Agnes Moorhead, Dolly Parton, Pol Pot, Agatha Christie, Joan Crawford, Golda Meir, Moe Howard, Chiang Kai-Shek, Aristotle Onassis, Gerald Ford, Elvis Pressley, John Lennon, John Wayne, Natalie Wood, Paul Robeson, Sal Mineo, Howard Hughes, Mao Zedong, Leonardo Davinci, Bing Crosby, Groucho Marx, Werner von Braun, Jimmy Carter, Maria Callas, Hamilton Jordan, John Cazale, Pope Pius VI Pope John Paul I, Susan Anton, Norman Rockwell, Ted Cassidy, Nelson Rockefeller, Vivian Vance, Colonel Sanders, Jesse Owens, Steve McQueen, Albert Hitchcock, Shah Pahlavi, Mae West, Jimmy Durante, Omar Bradley, Bob Marley, Joe Louis, Allan Ludden, Harry Chapin, Anwar Sadat, William Holden, Natalie Wood, John Belushi, Grace Kelly, Henry Fonda, Bette Davis, Jack Swigert, Karen Carpenter, Tennessee Williams, Jack Dempsey, Ronald Reagan, Muddy Waters, Dennis Wilson, Johnny Weissmuller, Ray Kroc, Madonna, Marvin Gaye, Ansel Adams, Richard Burton, Truman Capote, Indira Gandhi, Margaret Hamilton, Rock Hudson, Yul Brynner, Orson Wells, Paul Castellano, Roger Maris, Dian Fossey, Ricky Nelson, Christa McAuliffe, Judith Resnick, Michael Smith, Dick Scobee, Gregory Jarvis, Ellison Onizuka, Ronald McNair, Jimmy Cagney, Scatman Crothers, Cary Grant, Desi Arnaz, James Baldwin, Rita Heyworth, Fred

Astaire, Liberace, Lee Marvin, Jackie Gleason, Enzo Ferrari, John Mitchell, Roy Orbison, Hirohito, Salvador Dali, Ted Bundy, Lucille Ball, Laurence Olivier, Irving Berlin, Roald Dahl, Sarah Vaughan, Ava Gardner, Jim Henson, Alvin Alley, Sammy Davis Jr., Leonard Bernstein, Tyra Banks, Dr. Seuss, Miles Davis, gene Roddenberry, Freddie Mercury, Sam Walton, Copernicus, Newton, Alex Haley, Lawrence Welk, Bill Clinton, Mariah Carey, Toni Braxton, Whitney Houston, Julia Roberts, Al Gore, Denzel Washington, L.A. Reid, Katherine Hepburn, Thurgood Marshall, Andre the Giant, Audrey Hepburn, Arthur Ashe, Pablo Escobar, Vincent Price, Jeffrey Dahmer, Juvenal Habyarimana, Nicole Brown Simpson, Ron Goldman, Bert Lancaster, Wolfman Jack, Jerry Garcia, Dean Martin, Mickey Mantle, Joe Campbell, Dr. Jonas Salk. Bob Ross, Ella Fitzgerald, Princess Diana, Mother Teresa, Florence Joyner, Hillary Clinton, Chelsea Clinton, George Burns, Tiny Tim, Jon Benet Ramsey, Tupac Shakur, Jimmy Stewart, Gianni Versace, Jacques Cousteau, Celine Dion, Janet Jackson, Richard Dardis, Donald Trump, Joe Biden, Sonny Bono, Frank Sinatra, Barry Goldwater, Roy Rogers, Alan Shepard, Stanley Kubrick, Joe DiMaggio, Mario Puzo, John F. Kennedy Jr., George C. Scott,, Wilt Chamberlain, Walter Payton, Alec Guinness, Walter Matthau, Charles Schultz, Tom Landry, Derrick Thomas, Dale Earnhardt, Antony Quinn, George Harrison, Jack Lemmon, Dr. Christian Barnard, Aaliyah, Waylon Jennings, Johnny Unitas, Rod Steiger, Richard Harris, John Gotti, Ted Williams, Lacey and Connor Peterson, George W. Bush, John McCain, Alan Keyes, Johnny Cash, Gregory Peck, Mr. Fred Rogers, Bob Hope, Charles Bronson, Nina Simone, Johnny Carson, Ed McMahon, Marlon Brando, Ray Charles, Christopher Reeve, Pat Tilman, Francis Crick, Rosa Parks, Richard Pryor, Pope John Paul II, Pat Morita, Arthur Miller, James Brown, Coretta Scott King, Billy Preston, Saddam Hussein, Yvonne DeCarlo, Benazir Bhutto, Lady Bird Johnson, Luciano Pavarotti, Kurt Vonnegut, Evel Knevel, Heath Ledger, Paul Newman, George Carlin, Eartha Kitt, Charlton Heston, Patrick Swayze, Ted Kennedy, Farrah Fawcett, David Carradine, Walter Cronkite, Michael Jackson.

Many Thanks and respect to all the characters in book three of the 'Train of Thought' 'Dreams'. They are as follows and in order of appearance:

Taylor Swift, J.D. Salinger, Lena Horne, Dennis Hopper, Gary Coleman, John Wooden, Eddie Fisher, Gloria Stewart, Barbara Billingsley, Leslie Nielsen, Jill Clayburgh, Steve Jobs, Elizabeth Taylor, Joe Frazier, Bubba Smith, Christopher Stevens, Sean Smith, Tyrone Woods, Glen Doherty, Eta James, Whitney Houston, Mike Wallace, Donna Summer, Ray Bradbury, Andy Griffith, Sally Ride, Neil Armstrong, Michael Clarke Duncan, Adam Lanza, Nancy Lanza, The 26 wonderful adults and children from Sandy hook, Charlotte Bacon, Daniel Barden, Rachel D'Avino, Olivia Engel, Josephine Gay, Dylan Hockley, Dawn Lafferty Hochsprung, Madeleine Hsu, Catherine Hubbard, Chase Kowalski, Jesse Lewis, Ana Marquez-Greene, James Mattioli, Grace McDonnell, Anne Marie Murphy, Emilie parker, Jack Pinto, Noah Pozner, Caroline Previdi, Jessica Rekos, Avielle Richman, Lauren Rousseau, Mary Sherlach, Victoria Soto, Benjamin Wheeler, and Allison Wyatt. Barack Obama, Margaret Brewer, Stan Musial, Margaret Thatcher, Dr. Joyce Brothers, James Gandolfini, Scott Carpenter, Nelson Mandela, Phil Everly, Pete Seeger, Phillip Seymore Hoffman, Robin Williams, Shirley Temple, Maya Angelou, Joan Rivers, Ben Bradlee, The people at Charlie Hebdo, Rod Taylor, Ernie Banks, Leonard Nimoy, Robert Schuller, Leslie Gore, Michael Graves, John Nash, Omar Shariff, B.B. King, Louise Suggs, Yogi Berra, Natalie Cole, David Bowie, Glenn Frey, Prince, Harper Lee, Abe Vigoda, George Martin, Muhammed Ali, Elie Wiesel, Gene Wilder, Arnold Palmer, John Glenn, Mary Tyler Moore, Chuck Berry, Don Rickles, Helmut Kohl, Glen Campbell, Jerry Lewis, Hugh Hefner, Tom Petty, Fats Domino, Donald trump, Robert Mueller, Vic Damone, Billy Graham, Hubert de Givenchy, Stephen Hawking, Barbara Bush, Aretha Franklin, Kofi Annan, Bert Reynolds, George H.W. Bush, Frank Robinson, John Havlicek, Doris Day, Tim Conway, I.M. Pei, Gloria Vanderbilt, Toni Morrison, Blu, Gayle Sayers, Bob Gibson, Whitey Ford, Joe Morgan, Sean Connery, Alex Trebek, Pierre Cardin, Dawn Wells, Betty White, Desmond Tutu,

Cicely Tyson, Hank Aaron, Sarah Weddington, Michael Nesmith, Colin Powell, Ray Liotta, Naomi Judd, Thick Nhat Hanh, Michael Aday, Charles McGee, Sydney Poitier, Queen Elizabeth, Peter Bogdanovich, Kirstie Alley, Olivia Newton-John, James Caan, Burt Bacharach, Paco Rabanne, Cindy Williams, Barrett Strong, Bobby Hull, David Crosby, Gina Lollobrigida, Lisa Marie Pressley, Raquel Welsh, Richard Belzer, Tim McCarver, Ricou Browning, Barbara Bosson, Stella Stevens, Wayne Shorter, Tom Sizemore, Judy Heumann, Captain Smith, Liberace, Chaim Topol, Pat Schroeder, Lance Reddick, Willis Reed, Ryuichi Sakamoto, Benjamin Ferencz, Michael Lerner, and Mary Quant, Lenny Goodman, Harry Belafonte, Jerry Springer, Gordon Lightfoot, Tory Bowie, Vida Blue, Jim Brow, Tina Turner, Jacky Oh, Jim Hines, Astrud Gilberto, Francoise Gilot, Roger Payne, Treat Williams, Cormac McCarthy, and Dr. Martin Luther King Jr.

www.ingramcontent.com/pod-product-compliance
Lightning Source LLC
Chambersburg PA
CBHW020806310726
48969CB00002B/727